TO HELL WITH IT

Wicked Crown Book 3

MAY SAGE

ERIN BEDFORD

To Hell With It
Wicked Crown Book 3
May Sage & Erin Bedford © 2022
Edited by Makenzie Frazier
Cover by Sylvia Frost of The Book Brander
Boutique

❀ Created with Vellum

Roth

He remembered the first time he ever laid eyes on Lily Star Morgan. To be fair, Roth had felt her rather than seen her first.

Sitting at his favorite table in Unders while he pretended to be listening to some, she-demon prattle on about the ways she could make him feel good, Roth's skin came alive. It hadn't been a gradual thing, something that grew over time. One moment he was thinking of stabbing the knife by his plate into the she-demon's breast to see if it was real and the next, his whole body lit up.

Every neuron, every cell, every molecule had shot their shot, screaming at him all at once that she was here. This was his mate. This was the one he would spend eternity with.

Roth knew it down to his very being before she even stepped into his line of sight.

"What is it?" the she-demon, he had forgotten her name, asked him. Clearly feeling the same change in him as he had in that moment.

Roth ignored her, his amber eyes searching the crowded club. His gaze pushed around the demons, witches, and other beings alike until as if the sea of them were parting just for him, there she was.

Lily Star Morgan.

Hair a curly tangled mess of black and white, her stunning blue eyes skimmed the crowd with fascination and wariness. This was not a woman who trusted easily. And yet his best friend was leading her right to him.

Jealousy had buried into Roth's stomach instantly wondering what Ash had to do to get her to trust him. Had he flirted with her? Made her sweet promises? He swore to all that was unholy that if Ash had touched her, friend or not, he would kill him. For Roth knew as he locked the gaze of those curious eyes that she was his.

The crowd moved slowly as she came closer, revealing her shapely figure beneath the form fitting black dress she'd donned. He licked his lip while his gaze traveled down her magnificent legs barely concealed by the opaque tights she wore and down to the dark red ankle boots on her feet. He'd love nothing more in that moment than to worship at those very feet.

After waiting all this time, Roth thought he'd never have his mate. That he would be doomed forever to be alone and incomplete. With her walking toward him now it was as if the stars had aligned, and he finally knew why the humans referred to being in heaven so often.

When their gazes' locked Roth was glad to see that he was not the only one affected by the other's mere presence. Her body lurched slightly. Not enough that those around her would notice, only Roth who was watching her far more closely than he should have been. The moment she came within smelling distance, Roth's already hardening cock turned granite. The delectable heady scent of her arousal danced around him, begging him to come and take her, claim her right there in front of every supernatural being, the consequences be damned.

The she-demon next to him wrapped her arms around him, pulling at his attention as if to mark him as her own. Roth could not be wavered and the thrilling look of pure rage on the woman's face from the she-demon's attempts almost made him launch himself over the table in desire.

Barely restraining himself, Roth flipped the sniffer in his hand over and over, focusing on the movement rather than the thoughts of himself pounding in and out of his mate with rapid abandon.

"Come now, your highness, let me suck your cock. The she-demon purred in his ear, petting his silvery hair. "I'll do it right here in front of everyone if you like."

Roth never turned his gaze from her as he said, "I'd rather dip my cock in acid than have your touch anywhere near it."

The she-demon stiffened and then grumbled out a curse before leaving him blissfully alone to receive his mate and friend.

The woman saw the she-demon leave and smirked briefly, a small tug on those lovely lips that lasted only a second before she restrained her face, giving a short nod of consent as if knowing that Roth had dismissed the she-demon for her.

Ash placed his hand on her lower back, leading her toward him. Roth forced himself not to imagine ripping the offending thing off his friend for touching his mate. It wouldn't make the best first impression nor show his gratitude that the hellhound had found his mate in the first place.

"Roth—such a good surprise. What are you doing here, old man?"

Painful as it was, Roth ripped his gaze away from his mate to the hellhound. "This is my scene, Blackwell. You can find me in this dive more often than not." Roth watched with growing male satisfaction as she reacted to his voice. If her very insides quake at the sound of his voice, Roth could only contemplate the wondrous things he could do to her once he had his hands on her.

After a moment of thought, Roth offered her his hand.

She stared down at it for a moment before nodding her head and shaking it. The soft touch of her hand sent an electric shock that settled right into the base of his cock. Realizing he was staring, he released her hand and introduced himself, "Astaroth."

"The Great Duke of Hell," she smiled. Now he understood her reaction to his voice. Her own made him want to weep in joy. So, there was a God after all.

"That's a hell of a name to live up to."

Roth found himself smiling in return. Just a slight turn up of his lips. More of a smile than he had given anyone in over a hundred years. "So I hear, I go by Roth, in any case."

He found himself waiting with bated breath to hear the name of his mate. His one true and forever love. The one he had been searching for since Lucifer's imprisonment.

"Lily Star Morgan."

"You going to lay there all day or what?"

Roth's eyes blinked up at the voice above him. Fuck. Even that hurt. Ash leaned over him, his brow raised, and mouth twisted to the side, a smear of blood down the side of his face.

His lovely memory of meeting Lily for the first time drifted away, leaving him laying on the ground at the head of the battlefield, pain radiating through his body. Roth tried to move and failed. Each breath he took in was like razors in his lungs. He knew he couldn't stay there. He had to get up. He had to move. Lily needed him.

Roth assessed the pain in his body. Every inch of him felt like it was on fire. Which made sense. He had been blasted by that asshole Gabriel. Roth would give Gabriel pain in return tenfold. As soon as he could get up off the ground.

"I thought I might take a nap first," Roth grunted and shifted. Damn. He'd been hit good.

Ash blinked down at him. "You sure you're alright?"

Lifting his head, Roth shifted his head from one side to the other. Well, that worked. Next were his fingers and toes and when those worked, he lifted his hand up, placing it down on the ground to push himself up into a seated position. Roth raised his gaze to Ash, taking in the concerned look on his face. "Do I really look as bad as I feel?"

Ash snorted, "You look like you got hit by a massive blast of power so...I would guess so?" He tilted his head to the side, "Shouldn't we-" a shout from above made his head jerk up. Roth's eyes followed the path of Ash's gaze and widened.

His mate charged through the air welding two swords made of pure energy. Her wings were the most beautiful thing he had ever seen in his long life. He couldn't wait to touch them. Have them spread out above him as Lily rode his cock.

Roth winced. Now was not the time for that line of thought.

Roth's eyes followed his mate, locking onto the shining black crown on her head. Power pulsated from it encompassing Lily's aura with its wretched power. If Roth had his way, Lily would never take on the power of the Wicked Crown. He wouldn't wish the corrupted power on anyone. Especially not his mate. Seeing her with the gleaming black crown on her beautiful head made Roth's heart hurt. He ached for the mental torture she must be going through. The physical weight of the Wicked Crown may not be much. However, the weight on the psyche was almost impossible for anyone but royalty to bear.

"You know, your shield is about to come down," Ash reminded him, his gaze pinched with worry.

Grunting, Roth pushed up to a seated position. "Yes, unfortunately, I will not be able to keep it up much longer. Are you ready?" Roth glanced up at his friend.

Ash's eyes flashed gold and smoke billowed from his mouth as a wolfish grin curled up his lips. "To kick some angel ass? Of course! Are you going to be okay? Maybe you should sit this one out."

Roth gave Ash a pointed look. "I've been hit worse than this before and lived. I will be fine. Have you seen any sign of the others from Earth?"

Ash shook his head. "If they've come, I haven't seen them. But -" his head jerked to the side; his gaze caught on something further out. "Is that?" he stepped away from Roth, eyes squinting before his brows rose and a smile stretched across his face. "Well, I'll be damned."

"What?" Roth pushed up to his knees and then his feet. Each movement painstakingly slow. He followed Ash's line of sight. "Is that who I think it is?"

A familiar royal head of golden hair fought the surrounding angels, his magnificent power pushing dozens of them back at a time.

"Our king, yes," Ash nodded and then pursed his lips, a frown tugging down on his face. "If he's here then does that mean..."

Roth saw her first. Shooting a hand forward, Roth pointed toward the back of the horde. "Looks like our king is not alone in this battle."

Ash's gaze followed Roth's hand until they landed on Raven and what seemed to be her father, Michael, leading the charge against the back half of the angel horde. Roth could feel the relief coming off of Ash at seeing his mate back in one piece. It only lasted a brief moment before tension and anxiety caused his shoulders to bunch.

"I have to get out there," Ash turned his head back to Roth, practically vibrating with the need to move. "I have to help her."

Roth nodded, patting Ash on the shoulder. "Go, I'm fine. I'll lead the others forward. You go help your mate."

Ash clamped his hand on Roth's opposite shoulder, and they exchanged a meaningful look. No words were needed to express their gratitude for the others' friendship. We both knew what we meant to one another.

"Go, the shield is coming down one way or another."

Ash jerked his head once before turning, his flames and shadows moving over his body until it completely covered him. It was always interesting to see Ash change from man to beast. Sometimes Roth envied the freedom Ash's bestial form must give him.

Shaking his head to clear his mind, Roth turned his attention back to the task at hand. Bringing down the shield.

At this point he was surprised the angels hadn't broken through it already. The energy he had to expel to keep it up was almost gone and one more good blow would have brought it down on them.

Roth pivoted to the demons waiting behind him. They were scared and yet there was a fierce determination in their faces that made Roth proud.

"This is it, my brothers and sisters!" Roth called out walking across the front of the line. "This is where we make our stand. Our king is out there fighting right now." He pointed a finger toward where Lucifer battled the angels. "And our future queen battles above us." The demons' gazes lifted to the sky. "Do we let them fight for us alone?"

A thunderous roar responded.

"Then prepare yourselves." Roth twisted back around to the shield where the angels crashed against it like waves upon the shore. Roth closed his eyes and sucked in a breath, pulling the energy from the shield back into himself one piece at a time. When it was done, he opened his eyes and flashed a grin. "We fight!"

Lily

The Wicked Crown whispered in her mind as Lily scanned the legions of angels below her while she flew high above the Underworld.

It wanted her to wipe them all out. Right now. Make them all feel the pain that they'd caused Lily all her life.

It was their fault that her family had been broken. It was their fault that her parents left her to be raised by witches. She had been a freak amongst her own kind. Feeling like she never quite belonged...anywhere. All because she was different. Special.

Well, she'd show them exactly why they should fear her.

That's it. They deserve it. The Wicked Crown whispered in her head. *Take them. Take them all now.*

The boiling rage inside of her

pushed against her chest and the need to do some damage was almost too much to deny. The images of the girls that had died because they happened to look like her flashed through her head.

Those girls didn't deserve it. They hadn't deserved the gruesome deaths they'd been delivered by the hands of the angels. Neither had she...neither had...Lily swallowed thickly and kept her gaze away from the ground where Roth's injured form surely laid.

Straightening her shoulders, Lily focused on the task at hand. She would get retribution for them all. She'd make them all pay for what they'd done. But first...

Lily's wings beat against the air as if they had been there all her life. Flying should have been a life altering thing. Something she should have been able to experience with a smile on her face and laughter in her chest. With Roth and...her eyes flickered down to the ground where the King of Hell knelt in awe or fear...she wasn't quite sure.

It didn't matter. Not now anyway.

The knowledge that her father was before her now should have also been a joyous occasion. But when the Wicked Crown had whispered it in her ears, all it brought was annoyance.

Now Lucifer showed up? Now that she was on the brink of losing everything, did he deem her worthy of his presence. For all she cared, he could go back to wherever he came from. She didn't need his help. She didn't need anyone's help. Not now that she had the Wicked Crown.

"I should have known this day would come," the archangel, Gabriel, mused, flying from side to side before her. Like a fly that was in dire need of swatting.

While the battle raged down below, Lily's fight was there in the sky. The archangel before her was responsible for most of her pain and heartache. The one that would soon die by her hands as well.

"What day is that?" Lily smirked, tilting her head slightly so that her violet-colored hair fell over her shoulder. "Your death?"

Gabriel sniffed, not afraid of her as Lily had hoped. "So arrogant just like your father. It's no wonder you gave into the power of the Wicked Crown." Gabriel shifted his sword from one hand to the other, the flame gleaming in the sunlight as his eyes narrowed. "It's no matter, you'll die soon enough."

"That's what you think." Lily lifted her hand and pulled power into her palm, the sudden knowledge of what she needed to do coming as easily to her as breathing.

Normally, Lily would make a ball of fire. This time the power lengthened and stretched until it formed a sharp point, the bottom becoming a hilt in her hand. With a smile that was not at all pleasant, Lily grasped the sword she'd made in both hands. "Let's do this."

Hesitancy flashed on Gabriel's face. Just for a moment. It was enough to show Lily that he feared her finally. Enough to let her sink further into the clutches of the Wicked Crown, letting it fill her entire being with delicious power.

"You think you can beat me?" Gabriel scoffed with a jerk of his head toward her new sword. "With that pathetic excuse for a weapon? My power is far beyond anything you can dream of, little girl." He lifted his arms up to the sky, his sword a burning flame above him. "I hold the power of God himself in my hands and you come at me with a puny stick of light?" Throwing his head back and laughing, he didn't see Lily coming for him until it was almost too late.

Lily's weapon clashed with Gabriel's in a resounded boom that shook the air and radiated to the ground below them. The demons roared in protest as the angels shouted, charging against the shield of energy that wavered at their onslaught.

Hold on, Roth. Just a little longer.

"Do you think you can save them?" Gabriel hissed between their two weapons, "that you mean anything at all? This is nothing." He shoved against Lily's weapon, she grunted in effort pushing back with equal force. "You are *nothing*."

Lily's lips quirked up on one side. "Really now? I wouldn't say I'm nothing. After all, you did spend the last twenty years searching for me and destroying countless lives in the process. I would think that would make me a great big something. Don't you?" Lily cocked her head to the side and pursed her lips. "Or do you just have a huge crush on me? Can't get anyone to suck that tiny angel dick up in Utopia? Have to get your kicks killing little girls?"

Gabriel's eyes lit with rage, his teeth baring at her.

"Oh," Lily pouted mockingly. "Hit a nerve? That's okay. Soon you won't have any." Lily's smile was once again anything but nice. "Because you know, you'll be dead."

"You talk too much, little girl." Gabriel swiped out with his free hand, a dagger coming out of nowhere.

Lily shoved away from Gabriel, her wings beating fiercely as she put distance between them, aptly avoiding the dagger from plunging into her heart. Scowling at having to retreat, Lily surveyed Gabriel who didn't try to come after her.

"Coward!" she tossed at the archangel. "Afraid I'll cut your dick off? Of course, that would require you to have one to begin with."

Gabriel didn't take the bait.

With a mischievous grin, Lily held her energy sword in one hand while producing another one in the other hand. Now with a sword in both hands, Lily said, "Fine. Won't come to me, then I'll come to you."

Lily's wings pushed through the air as she shot toward the retreating archangel. The fight below them had begun with Lucifer and what looked like...Michael? And Raven? Attacking from both sides.

A part of her was ecstatic that her friend was back and alright, while the other part sneered at her bad timing. Where was the Nephilim before this all happened? She had taken her precious time showing up when they needed her before

Gabriel twisted and turned in the air dodging the attacks Lily threw his way. Dickless had the audacity to laugh at her. "Look at you, you can't even keep up. Haven't got the hang of your wings yet, child?"

The Wicked Crown crooned in Lily's ear. *Take him out. You can do it. Just one burst of power and you can wipe them all out at once.*

Lily shook her head. She couldn't. If she did that then what was keeping her from killing all of her people too?

"If you'd stand still then this would all be over," Lily snapped back at him and swiped both swords through the air sending an x-shaped energy blast toward the smirking Gabriel. To her violent delight, he didn't move fast enough to dodge it completely. The blast burned through the upper side of Gabriel's armor.

Gabriel hissed and cursed, glaring at the burning flesh. "Is that the best you can do?"

Prepping for another attack, Lily didn't let Gabriel's taunting faze her. Before she could release the buildup of energy, the shield around the palace flickered and then all at once disappeared. Lily's heart jumped in her chest at what that meant.

Roth.

"Uh-oh," Gabriel chuckled darkly. "Looks like it's over for your hellspawn now."

The moment the shield fell the angels surged forward and swarmed over the small amount of demon forces they had mustered. Lily was torn between helping her people and beating down the archangel in front of her who was responsible for her life going to shit.

"Save your precious demons or come after me..." Gabriel crooned. A portal materialized behind him, and Gabriel moved through it, his words trailing after him. "What ever shall you do?"

Lily glanced to the portal and then back down at the ground. They needed her help. If she left them then they would be overtaken for sure. It seemed even with Gabriel gone that the angels weren't going to stop any time soon. Not unless another archangel stepped up to stop them.

She searched for Michael. Except trying to find one archangel in a sea of angels was like looking for a needle in a haystack.

Fuck!

Lily turned away from the portal, the Wicked Crown raging in her head to turn back and take her revenge. Shoving the voice away, Lily flexed her fingers around the swords in her hands and charged into the fray.

Raven

Swinging a spear she had stolen from one of the angels, Raven swiped it across the air. It caught several angels in its arc, knocking them back. With her spare hand she shot an energy blast out, pushing the fray even further away from her.

Shit. There were too many. How was she going to get to the front lines with all of Utopia between her and them? Raven's gaze shot to where Lily fought Gabriel in the sky. She wanted nothing more than to get up there and take a piece out of the archangel who had spent years torturing her.

"How are you faring, daughter?" Michael landed a few feet away from her, protecting her back from oncoming attacks. His long black hair swung around him as he spun just above the ground, blowing a blast of air at the angels who dared come up against him.

Raven stabbed the pointed end of the spear through a charging angel and grunted out, "Never better. I hope you have a plan because I don't see us getting through this one on our own."

Michael grabbed two angels and smashed their heads together. His movements more effortless than Raven's. Perhaps if she hadn't been so proud, she would have been able to learn how to do that long before now. They could have worked on her form and powers together, making them the most fearsome father-daughter team in either Utopia or the Underworld.

Rubbing the sweat from her brow, Raven shook her head. Now wasn't the time for regret. There would be plenty of time to make up for it later. They just had to get through this first.

Catching her off guard, an angel broke through her defenses knocking her to the ground. They pounced on her. Raven struggled to throw the irritating angel off of her. "Michael, a little help here," she called out to her father, her head tilting back to find him, but he was in the middle of his own fight and couldn't get to her.

"Fuck," she ground out, pushing

her spear against the angel, her biceps shouting in protest. "Get the fuck off of me."

"Die, traitor!" the angel hissed, stabbing at the air before her. The dagger lashed out faster than she could stop it and it sliced across her cheek. Blood leaked down her face. Thankfully the slow pour told her the cut wasn't deep enough to worry about. She only hoped it wouldn't scar too much.

As she fought against the angel, a bone numbing roar filled the air causing the angel's head to turn to the side seconds before he was thrown off of her.

Eyes following the angel, Raven's heart jumped in her throat at seeing the hellhound ripping the angel apart. Unfortunately, Raven didn't have time to count her blessings before she was back on her feet fighting against another group of angels, this time with Ash at her back.

"Took you long enough," she teased at the beast behind her. Ash huffed behind her. "Hey, don't bring me excuses. You left me there with Michael when you could have stayed."

An angel cried out as Ash threw him across the field. An arm grabbed Raven around the waist. She swung out to attack and came face to face with Ash, his hand on her wrist to keep her from hitting him. "Don't be mad, Raven. I thought you were safe with your dad." His eyes narrowed in on the cut on her cheek and a low growl trickled out of his lips. "I'll kill him."

Body pressed up against his, Raven found it hard not to react to Ash's closeness even though they were in the middle of a battlefield. Rolling her eyes at his words, Raven jerked a hand toward the dead angel, "Already taken care of and you're changing the subject. You know, that's not the point."

A few angels took that moment to attack them. Ash grabbed Raven's spear and skewered them through the middle and shoved them back into the crowd before pulling her close once more. "Oh," Ash flicked her chin with a wolfish grin. "Did you miss me?"

Raven's lower lip pushed out as she ground out, "Not really. And I was using that spear."

Ash smirked and tugged on her at her lower lip. "You're a bad liar." He jumped onto the back of an angel and snapped his neck, grabbing the spear in his limp hands. Ash tossed it to her. "Here, don't say I never got you anything."

"And you're a self-centered-" Raven

shot back, pushing away from Ash to kick an angel in the face before turning back to Ash, "-asshole."

"Ouch, Raven," Ash placed a hand on his chest with a pained look. "Ouch."

Rolling her eyes at his theatrics, Raven twisted out of his grasp to focus on the angels coming at them. "You know, this is not the time or place."

Fighting his own angels, Ash retorted, "You're the one who brought it up. I'm simply defending myself."

Raven snorted, kicking an angel in the face before punching another one. Between hits she panted out, "You're just too much of a coward to admit that you didn't want to face my father."

Ash shoved off three angels and spun around, huffing with breath before her. "That is neither here nor there. I thought you were dead. I searched for you for years, Raven. Years! Do you have any idea how it felt?"

Raven shoved the end of the spear into another angel who clawed at the end while she said, "I was a little busy being tortured so no...I don't." She propped her foot up on the angel's shoulder and shoved, pulling the spear with her hands.

"Well, I do." Ash grabbed her arm,

his other holding a stolen sword. "Every second you were gone was like razor blades in my lungs. I couldn't breathe. I couldn't sleep. I wanted so badly to find you. To save you and it killed a little bit of me every day you were away from me."

A fist clenched around Raven's heart at Ash's words. "I'm sorry, I didn't realize my capture affected you so much." Her gaze softened at the strain on Ash's face. She opened her mouth to tell him how much she missed him too. Before she could get it out Michael dropped next to them with a glower.

"Can you two converse at a later time?" Michael fought off two angels at once before blowing back a group of them with his wings. "Perhaps when we aren't wings deep in enemies?"

Raven hated to admit that her father was right. Now was not the time for this particular conversation. Returning her attention to the task at hand, Raven put all her efforts into fighting to stay alive rather than Ash's presence. A second after stabbing another angel through the neck all the angels paused as if they had all been signaled at once. Their eyes turned to the sky.

Curiosity pulled Raven's gaze to the sky as well.

Squinting up at the air, Raven made out Lily's violet hair and her new wings. Then she found the thing that had drawn the angels' attention in the first place.

A portal appeared in the middle of the sky and the familiar form of one archangel, Gabriel, went through it.

"Gabriel is fleeing," Ash crowed with a whoop. "The bastard couldn't take the heat."

Raven agreed but worried more about what to do with the angels Gabriel had left behind. Would they stay and fight or flee with their boss?

Raven turned to Michael. "Can you send the other angels back?" Her words caused the angels nearest to them to turn their way. Her fingers tightened around the spear, prepared to be attacked once more.

However, Michael's wings flapped, and he took up to the sky and when his voice called out the power poured out with it, "Leave this place now."

The angels hesitated.

They looked around at each other and then to us. Some of them seem to be fighting the need to obey Michael's orders, taking a step toward us. Then Michael's powers pushed out once more. "Leave now."

That was all they needed before

they reluctantly took to the sky. The whole horde moved at once. Raven watched with a bit of awe and fear as thousands of angels flew away as if nothing had happened.

"Well," Ash huffed, swiping his brow. "That's one way to win a war."

Michael leveled his gaze on us. "We may have won this battle, but it is far from over."

Lucifer

The misguided angels flew away leaving Lucifer on the ground bleeding and barely able to stand. The fight back in Utopia had taken more out of Lucifer than he thought. Thankfully, Gabriel was as much of a coward as he had been all his life. Lucifer knew once Gabriel went up against his daughter with the full power of the Wicked Crown behind her that he would take the easy way out.

However, that only meant they had a small reprieve before Gabriel was back trying to destroy them all. Though, he was most likely to try and take Lily out before he tried again. A blessing and a possible problem to worry about later.

"My king," a demon knelt at his

side, a fist to his chest. "It is good to have you back."

Lucifer nodded and grimaced, not trying to move more than he had to.

Another few demons surrounded him. Some looked at him with disbelief and relief. While others, confusion. Lucifer supposed his sudden appearance would be baffling for some. Others probably had no idea who he even was.

"Do you need assistance, my king?" the first demon asked, glancing at the blood seeping from Lucifer's wing. "You, help His Majesty get up. We need to get him to the palace."

The demon in question hesitated before moving toward him. Lucifer tensed as the demon tried to find some way to help him without hurting him more.

"Stop that. Don't touch him." The order came from the side and from a voice Lucifer recognized. The demon stopped what he was doing at the command.

Lucifer turned his head to the side as much as he could without causing pain to his wings. "Astaroth. Good to see that you're still alive. Though, I'd have preferred it in much different circumstances." Lucifer grunted and tried to twist his body to face the demon prince. "Thank you for finding my daughter."

Astaroth moved into Lucifer's line of view, his own body as battered and bruised as Lucifer's. "I promised I would find her, and I won't break my promises." Astaroth knelt before Lucifer, his watchful eyes scanning over Lucifer's form. "I'm just sorry I didn't find her sooner."

Lucifer snorted. "I shouldn't have been stupid enough to believe a word out of that asshole of a brother of mine."

Astaroth's lips ticked up at the sides and he laughed.

"What?" Lucifer tilted his head to the side, the movement making him wince.

Shaking his head, Astaroth pushed to his feet. "Nothing. Lily is just so much like you."

"She is?" Lucifer's gaze followed Astaroth's movements. "I'd like to meet with her." His eyes lifted to the sky, but his daughter was no longer flying up above.

Astaroth bobbed his head. "Understandable. First, let's get you taken care of." He snapped his fingers at several demons. "You three...help our returning king...carefully...up to the palace. Bring him to the infirmary. We can assess the damage there." He shifted to leave.

"Astaroth."

The demon prince turned back to Lucifer with an expectant look. "Yes, my king?"

"We're going to have to talk about that mate bond."

Astaroth smirked, his eyes glinting dangerously. "No, we don't. She's mine as much as I am hers. There's nothing to talk about."

Annoyance at being defied pinched Lucifer's face but he let the topic drop for now with a nod of his head. Astaroth pivoted on his heel and moved through the crowd assessing the damage done to their people.

It seemed in the time Lucifer was gone that Astaroth had taken up the mantle as leader to his people. The demons moved aside for Astaroth as he moved through the crowd, and he greeted each of them as if they were equal to him and not lowly cannon fodder. Lucifer could see the loyalty and love in their eyes for Astaroth, something Lucifer used to have from the demons. Now they didn't seem to know what to think of their king.

Though, was he still a king when the Wicked Crown was on his daughter's head?

"Come, Your Majesty." One of the demons held out his arms to Lucifer and the other two oh so carefully helped Lucifer to his feet, bracing his wings so they didn't drag on the ground behind him as they made the arduous trek back to the palace.

Yes, there were many things that had changed since Lucifer had let himself be imprisoned. Many mistakes had been made on his part that must be corrected. However, leaving Astaroth in charge had not been one of them.

Lily

R age burned through Lily as she watched the retreating back of Gabriel. She wanted nothing more than to go after the archangel and yet she pulled away from the demons down below about to be slaughtered by the angel masses.

When the angels below realized Gabriel was gone, they paused. Further enraging Lily and the Wicked Crown who wanted to devour everything in its sights. Then Michael called out a command to leave. Even Lily felt the command in her bones though it had no pull on her actions.

The angels took to the sky, fleeing now that their leader was no longer there to back them up. The sight of them zooming through the skies of

Hell made Lily's fingers curl into fists around the swords in her hands. She should take them out now. Get rid of them before Gabriel could regather his forces and try again.

Prepping to charge at the retreating angels, Lily didn't notice the other angel swooping toward her until the black-haired girl was in her face.

"Lily!" Raven's voice came out a gasping croak. "You...you have wings!"

Jerking her eyes away from the retreating forces with much effort, Lily's gaze landed on Raven's hovering form. Unclenching her hands, Lily allowed the power to be pulled back into herself. Waste not, want not.

"It would seem so," Lily replied dryly. "I see you have survived Gabriel's captivity." She skimmed the angel briefly before shifting her gaze back to the angels which were quickly disappearing back the way they came.

Raven grabbed Lily by the shoulders and pulled her into a tight hug. "Oh my god, you have no idea what's happened. Gabriel was just..." she let out a shaky breath. "I can't really talk about it."

"I can imagine," Lily muttered into Raven's shoulder. She stiffly let Raven hold her wondering when she would be released. "You found my father it seems."

Raven withdrew from Lily and gazed down at the ground. "Yes, I did." Her brows furrowed, her head jerking back up to Lily. "How did you know he was your father?"

Lily clucked her tongue in distaste. "It's kind of hard to deny it when so many things were being shoved into my face." She flicked her violet-colored hair over her shoulder, drawing attention to the black crown on her head. "It would be superfluous to think otherwise at this point. It's pretty obvious where I belong." Her wings flapped behind her as if to remind her that they were there. Another prime clue of her parentage.

Turning her attention back to the ground, Lily drawled, "Where is my father anyway?"

Shifting a bit lower, Raven led her down to the ground. "Last I saw he was over in that direction," her hand pointing toward the central area of the battle ground. Lily was disappointed to see that there were more fallen demons than angels on the field. The demons weren't even close to being ready for this kind of attack. They had become complacent - weak - in their exile. Something they would have to remedy before the next attack.

And there would be one. Lily had no doubt in her mind that Gabriel would find some way to come at them again. Though, this time it might not be a frontal attack. She'd have to watch her back and all other sides of her.

"It must be confusing seeing your dad for the first time."

Lily landed on the ground, and she suddenly felt the loss of the wind on her face and the air pushing up her wings. She shifted her wings behind her. "Why would you think that? As far as I'm concerned, I didn't need him when he was playing in heaven, I don't need him now."

"Ouch," Raven's nose scrunched up. Her wings disappeared.

Lily had to figure out how to do that. She pushed her wings behind her and hoped they disappeared into some kind of pocket. But no luck.

"That's a bit harsh don't you think?" Raven placed her hands on her hips and scowled at Lily. "As soon as he found out you were alive and here, Lucifer broke out of his cell and took on dozens of angels and an archangel just to get to you. To see you. Help you." She said the last bit slowly as if Lily couldn't understand her without it.

"He shouldn't have wasted his time." Lily squinted in concentration opening and shutting her wings, trying in earnest to put her wings away. "I obviously don't need or want his help." She growled and threw her hands up in a huff, giving up.

"Lily," Roth growled, stalking toward her, breaking through the dispersing demons. "I could throttle you for what you did." He grabbed her arms and pulled her in, holding her to him tightly. She inhaled the scent of him and sank into his embrace. After a moment, he pulled away and stared down at her with concern in his eyes. "Taking on the Wicked Crown in this state was extremely dangerous. You could have been killed the moment you put it on."

Lily pushed away from him, lifting her hands in front of her. "As you can see, I'm fine. Better than ever even." Lily smirked and fluttered her wings behind her. "I've even evolved to my final form. No thanks to some people." Lily's gaze trailed behind Roth to where Lucifer was being helped up the steps by a couple of lower demons.

The angel before her was nothing like what she had imagined her father would look like. In fact, Lily had tried hard not to think about what her father was like before he abandoned her. It had been one of the things that had gotten her through her childhood and teen years. He didn't want her, so she didn't want him.

Seeing the broken and beaten angel coming toward her should have caused some kind of emotion in her. Some kind of desire to help him. Even if he wasn't her father. However, all she felt was...disdain.

When Lucifer reached the top of the stairs, the demons lowered him before her and crept away. The urge to walk away from the archangel itched at her feet. She stomped the need down defiantly refusing to give him the satisfaction of seeing her uncomfortable.

"Lily," Lucifer breathed out, his blue gaze sweeping over her, taking in every detail. His voice was clear and felt like what some might call a warm hug. "I...I don't know how to express how sorry I am for not coming sooner. Oh, you..." He stepped toward her; a hand lifted toward her face. Lily jerked back from his touch. With a sad sigh, Lucifer dropped his hand. "...you just look so much like your mother."

"Save the nostalgia for someone who cares," Lily sneered.

"Lily!" Raven gasped, her eyes

shifting back and forth between the two of them.

Lily stepped forward until she was in Lucifer's personal bubble. "Let me make something clear. As far as I'm concerned, you're too little too late." Shoulders back and wings flared out behind her, Lily spoke loud and clear, "I rule Hell now and you will do well to stay out of my way."

The silence that followed her announcement did nothing to disway her. In fact, the look of fear and awe on the faces of the demons around her only spurred her on more. The Wicked Crown whispered in her head that this was it. This was what true power felt like.

"Lily," Roth took a cautious step in her direction, his hands out toward her but not touching her again. "Perhaps it's time to take off the Wicked Crown." His eyes flicked to the black crown on her head and then back to her face.

"Why?" Lily moved away from him, pushing her wings so that they lifted her off the ground. "So you can be on top again?" She shook her head, "I don't think so."

"Seriously Lily," Roth tried to convince her once more, "you aren't acting yourself. The Wicked Crown is making you this way."

"I don't know what you mean. I feel..." Lily's wings lifted her higher off the ground. "...free and more myself than I have felt in my whole life." She let the feeling creep up her face in a smirk. "Now if you'll excuse me, I have subjects needing tending to and a war to plan."

Roth

❧

"Don't beat yourself up over it," Lucifer reassured him as they watched Lily fly away. "Even if she took the Wicked Crown off now it wouldn't matter. The crown already has its claw in her."

Roth's frown deepened. "What do you mean? She's going to be like that all the time now?"

Lucifer shook his head, wincing when the gesture caused him pain. "I honestly don't know. It depends on her force of will and whether or not it is enough to fight back the influence of the Wicked Crown's power." He paused and stared off at nothing for a moment before adding, "It was locked away for a reason."

Lucifer would know. He'd had the Wicked Crown at one point. Though,

Roth never knew when or why he had taken it off.

"We can't just take the Wicked Crown away and throw it into a volcano or something?" Raven offered up hopefully.

Lucifer chuckled, the pinching at his eyes showing the pain he was in. "I wish it were that easy. However, the Wicked Crown is near indestructible and the longer my daughter wears it the more it will wear on her. You'd have to take the Wicked Crown from her for a long time to get it's..." Lucifer wiggled his hand in the air searching for the word.

"Bad juju?" Raven supplied.

Lucifer bobbed his head. "In a manner of speaking." Letting out a long sigh that made his wings twitch in a way that Roth knew had to be painful, Lucifer stared after where Lily had flown away. "I'm afraid only a long period of detox would get the Wicked Crown's influence out of her and that's if she allows you to have it."

The ground rumbled beneath them as Ash galloped over to them, scraping his claws into the ground as he came to a stop. Smoke curled around him, and the hellhound morphed back into his human form.

"So, what are we doing?" Ash peered around our tense group.

"Trying to figure out how to get the Wicked Crown away from Lily before she destroys herself and everyone else," Raven helpfully provided, shifting closer to Ash.

Ash cracked his knuckles and grinned. "Oh, I don't think that'll be a problem. All three of us and two archangels?" He waved a hand toward where Michael was making his way to\them. "Should be more than enough to take one little piece of metal from Lily."

Raven scoffed. "I think you underestimate Lily."

"And I think you overestimate her. She could barely throw fireballs without that crown. She can hardly be that much more powerful now. Right?" Ash turned his eyes to Roth. "Back me up here, Roth."

Roth turned his gaze from where Lily's shadow had faded. "You've been gone a while my friend. Lily has grown into her own even without the Wicked Crown. I think we should all be on our guard and try our best not to trigger her. We do not know if the Wicked Crown will see us as friend or foe."

"There is more to worry about than our own," Michael commented, stepping into their group. "We still have Gabriel and his angelic army to deal with."

"What?" Ash brushed a thumb over his nose. "Your command was not enough to keep them away?"

Michael gave Ash a pointed look. "The angels may listen to me when their leader is not around, but I am not all powerful. There is a hierarchy in such things."

"So, you're saying that you have no pull over them whatsoever when their daddy is in the picture?" Raven smartly pointed out.

Michael's lips tugged down in a frown. "I wouldn't say that exactly."

Raven opened her mouth to retort. Lucifer jumped in first.

"As fascinating as all this is to talk about in the middle of the battlefield where I'm not exactly sure we won, could we perhaps move this inside?" Lucifer grunted and wavered on his feet. "Maybe the infirmary?"

Raven's eyes widened. "Oh, crap. Sorry. I forgot. Here let me." She rushed to Lucifer's side and pulled his arm over her shoulders and then gestured to Ash. "Help me out here."

Ash moved to do her bidding almost too quickly. Roth wondered if Raven knew how much she had Ash wrapped around her finger. If she didn't, she would figure it out soon enough. Roth did not envy the hellhound.

Roth lingered behind with Michael as the other three inched toward the palace.

Michael watched them leave with a sort of pained look in his eyes. "Do you think she will ever rush to help me in such a way?"

Roth shrugged. "Who knows? Women are mercurial creatures. Even after all these centuries I am still finding myself flummoxed by them."

Smiling slightly, Michael inclined his head. "I understand that very well. Raven's mother was a fascinating and complicated woman and yet I find myself unable to connect with the one thing that means more than anything in the world to me."

"Perhaps, that is somewhere to start." Roth offered up. "Show Raven that you care and be there for her. Eventually, she will see that you are not like the other uncaring archangels and actually want to try."

"I can only pray that you are correct." Michael moved forward and then paused. "Though, I'm not sure my place is here and not back in Utopia.

Perhaps, I should be there to spy on the enemy?"

Roth chuckled. "I never thought I'd see the day when an archangel would be worried about the opinion of a measly Nephilim."

Michael shot him a glare. "My daughter is not just any Nephilim. And I find offense in the implications."

Roth nodded. "My apologies. No offense meant. Shall I show you to a guest room or..." Roth surveyed the archangel for injury. "Do you need to go to the infirmary?"

"No, I don't think I am injured in that manner." Michael's gaze took on that faraway look that Roth knew only too well.

Clapping a hand on the archangel's shoulder, Roth ushered him forward. "To that I'll have a large glass of the finest brandy in all of Hell."

Raven

Once she and Ash had deposited Lucifer in the infirmary, she followed him out of the room and into the hallway. Arms crossed over her chest, she stared down at the ground and leaned against the nearby wall.

"Do you think he'll be okay?"

Ash leaned a shoulder against the wall next to her. "Who? Lucifer? He's an archangel. There's no way that will kill him. I mean, those guys can take an ass load of punches and keep on going."

Raven chuckled.

"There's a smile." Ash brushed her hair behind her ear. "I thought I'd never see it again."

Blinking up at Ash, Raven asked, "Why would you think that?"

Ash's lip tugged down at the sides,

and he dragged a hand through his hair, a self-conscious look coming over his face. "You know, after...after what happened to you in Utopia. I thought I would never see you again. And I tried, Raven. I tried to find you..." He turned suddenly and punched the wall before leaning his forehead against the same wall with a dejected sigh. "I failed you."

Raven placed her hand on his arm and urged him to turn to her. "No, you didn't. You did everything you could."

"But...I could have done more."

"What are you? God?" Raven cupped his face between her hands and peered into his green eyes. "I never expected you to save me. The fact that you spent all this time trying makes me feel..." she trailed off, swallowing down the emotion that had billowed into her chest.

Ash shifted closer to Raven. She could feel his warm breath on her face, and it caused things down low to tighten. The knowledge that Ash was supposedly her mate was not the same thing as having it thrust into her face like this. They'd never actually...done anything about it. They hadn't had time...and yet...they had time now.

"Makes you feel...?" Ash prompted, his fingers curling against her side lightly.

Raven's tongue darted out to wet her lips. "You know...things."

Ash's lips curled at the edges, giving him a more houndish look than human. "What kind of things?"

Raven dropped a hand down to his shirt, watching as she twisted the material around her finger. "You know, the kind that makes me want to rip all your clothes off and do extremely biblical things with you."

Ash threw his head back and laughed, startling Raven. Gripping her by the back of the neck, Ash pulled her so close their lips brushed each other. "Oh, little angel, there is nothing biblical about the things I want to do to you. In fact, they are downright hellish."

Raven grinned against his lips. "Bring it on."

They barely made it down the hallway before Raven shoved Ash into a broom closet. She didn't give him time to ask questions before she jumped on him, wrapping her legs around his waist and latching her mouth to his.

Ash growled low in his chest, vibrating against her while cupping her ass. Raven ground down against the hardness she felt between them, groaning at the friction it caused. Ash lapped at her mouth, nipping and tasting every inch of her. Raven couldn't get enough of him. She wanted more. Needed it. Right now.

When her hands went to Ash's pants, he suddenly pulled back, grabbing her hands. "Hold up, wait a second, Raven."

Brows furrowed; Raven frowned at him. "What? Don't you want to...?"

"No, I mean...yes. I do. Very much so. But..." Ash released her hands and brushed her hair behind her ear in a gentle gesture that was completely the opposite of what they had just been doing. "I didn't imagine our first together would be a quick fuck in the broom closet."

Raven's expression softened. "You thought about what our first time would be like?" The idea of it made her heart skip a beat.

Ash gave her a boyish grin. "Well, yeah. You have no idea how often I thought about you while searching for you. How often I'd imagine having you beneath me or even above me while I came all over my hand." His cheeks flushed with embarrassment. It made her want to kiss him senseless.

"And none of those times were in a broom closet?"

Ash blinked at her. "No. They

weren't. Though, there was one time when I imagined bending you over your kitchen island and plowing into you from behind while Roth and Lily were in the other room."

Oh my. Raven's mouth went dry. She wanted that. She wanted him. Anyway she could get him. And if that meant letting him act out his perfect fantasy of their first time then she would give him exactly that and more.

Drooping her legs from around his waist, she grabbed his hand.

"Where are we going?" Ash asked, allowing her to lead him out of the broom closet and back into the hallway.

Raven tossed him a coy little grin over her shoulder. "To make all your fantasies come true. Starting with your first one. Which I'm assuming is in your bedroom?"

Ash squeezed her hand in response. "How do you know where you're going?"

"I don't but I figured you'd tell me where to go. After all, this is your fantasy."

Ash huffed a laugh. "God if I'm dreaming, please don't let me wake up any time soon."

Raven chuckled in response.

Lily

"How in all of Hell is there not one map of Utopia!" Lily shouted to the empty room. This was supposed to be in a war room at some point. A large round table sat in the middle of the room; a 3D map of Hell decorated the surface. She shuffled through piles of papers and rolls of parchment in search of something to help her.

Lily shifted her shoulders feeling weird without the weight of her wings on her back. She supposed it would take some getting used to. Though, it was nice to have finally figured out how to put the huge things away.

The door clicked open behind her, and she didn't need to look up from what she was doing to know it was her mate. "How am I supposed to plan my attack without the information I need?"

When he didn't answer right away, Lily lifted her head to meet his cautious gaze.

"If you would only tell me what you need my mate, I would be happy to provide it for you." Roth stayed on the other side of the room, his hands open at his sides as if he were showing her he wasn't a threat. The sight of it made something in her heart twinge.

Sighing, Lily drew a hand over her face and slouched forward over the piles of paper. "I'm not sure what I need. I just have this...this overwhelming need to...to do something." Her fingers clenched into fists as she pushed up from the table. "Do you know what I mean?"

Roth nodded, slowly moving around the table. His hand trailed over the tops of the chairs as he made his way over to her. Lily watched him with as much awe and want as she had the first time she'd seen him in that club with Ash. Except this time, she wasn't afraid to take what she wanted.

Lily stalked toward Roth, feeling every bit the bad ass she no doubt looked in those leathers Bacchi had squeezed her into.

Reaching up, she grabbed Roth by that gorgeous head of his and claimed his mouth as her own in a clash of teeth and tongues.

To Roth's credit he didn't balk away from this violent side of her. He pushed back with as much as she gave. A carnal thrill raced through Lily. She'd never felt so uninhibited. So powerful. So...free.

Her hands found their way under his shirt, his armor having been discarded somewhere else. She raked her nails down the hard lines of his abs wanting to rub herself all over his delectable form until he smelled like nothing else but her.

Roth moved forward, pushing them between two chairs until her hips hit the lip of the table.

Grinning, Lily worked at the belt of her pants and then growled in frustration at all the straps and hooks.

"Here," Roth replaced her hands with his. "Let me."

The demon prince had her pants undone and at her ankles in the next heartbeat. And then in the next, her naked ass on the table and her thighs spread wide, baring her wet heat to his hungry gaze.

Locking eyes with her, Roth kneeled before her. "You beat back Gabriel." He kissed the inside of her thigh.

"Yes," she gasped at the sensation. The anticipation of what was to come, making her squirm.

"You took on the Wicked Crown all because you feared for me." Another kiss. This time closer to her pulsating need.

Swallowing, Lily breathed, "I'd do anything for you."

Roth paused over her, blowing cool air on her hot skin. Lily's hips jerked up in response. A devilish grin on his lips, Roth commanded, "Then come for me, my queen."

The command would have made the Wicked Crown lash out at him had it not been accompanied by my queen. The Wicked Crown liked that. It liked it a lot. Almost more than Lily enjoyed the sight of Roth between her thighs.

Roth slid his tongue up the length of her, circling around her sensitive nub.

"Almost," Lily stuttered out, her eyes squeezing closed.

"That's it." Roth pushed two fingers into her without warning, cranking her pleasure up even further. "Let it go."

Lily didn't bother to explain to him that she wasn't talking about being close to the edge though now that he was doing that magical thing with his fingers she wasn't far off. She tried to spread her legs further and found herself trapped by her pants. Jerking at her legs with growing frustration, she brought power into her hands and burned through the material on her legs.

Roth pulled back and glanced down at her ankles, a curious frown on his face. "Well, that's one way to do it."

Lily grinned, "Yeah, it's nifty having all my powers readily available. Now... get back to it." She pulled at his hair, trying to find that edge she was so close to.

Instead of returning between her legs, Roth wrapped his fingers underneath her knees and jerked her forward until she laid on her back. Normally she'd be happy to see where this was going but there was the little fact that the table was not a flat surface.

Her head bumped against the top of what felt like a mountain top. "Hey now, as much as I like where this is going, I think I'm going to get a concussion if we do it here."

"Well, perhaps you would be more comfortable if you took your crown off." Roth's eyes slid to her head.

Lily reached up to her head. Before she touched the Wicked Crown her eyes narrowed, and she dropped her hand. "Wait a second. Is this what this is all about?"

"What, what is what all about?"

Pushing up on her elbows, Lily reluctantly withdrew her legs from Roth's grasp, suddenly regretting having destroyed her pants in a moment of passion. "You suddenly going down on me and all this my queen stuff."

Roth locked eyes with her and it was the intensity of that stare that made her doubt him for the first time since they'd met.

"I do not know what you mean, Lily." Except Roth stepped back from her and that one movement said more than anything he could ever say.

Lily shoved off the table and stalked toward him. "Are you trying to take the Wicked Crown from me?"

Roth crossed his arms over his chest, his lips pursing into a thin line.

"You are," Lily bared her teeth at him in a snarl. "You think I can't handle it. Don't you? That it's too much for poor little Lily Morning Star and I should just give it back. Well, let me tell you something, Prince Astaroth," She shoved her finger into his chest, trying to be as authoritative as one could be bare assed, "I am a grown woman who can make her own decisions and I don't need a man deciding when I am ready for anything."

Power built in her chest. Rage and disappointment raced through her veins. So overwhelmed with emotion Lily wanted to blow a hole through something, anything. Even the man that she loved.

That thought was like a bucket of cold water had been dumped on top of her. Using all her will power, she pushed the power away until all that was left was her frozen in fear at what she almost did.

Wrapping her arms around herself, Lily blinked down at the ground, tears building up behind her lashes. "Roth," she whispered, the shame in her chest keeping her from looking up at him. "I think I need help."

Warm hands wrapped around her shoulders and drew her close to a familiar chest. She breathed in her mate's scent and sank into his embrace as Roth petted her hair. "I've got you, Lily. I'm here."

Lucifer

The infirmary had gotten better than the last time Lucifer had frequented it. Though, that hadn't been often. As the king of Hell not many wanted to go toe to toe with him. It seemed Raven was right. He was rusty. All that time locked away had really weighed on his abilities.

That was then. Now, he was free and had a daughter to protect. Lucifer couldn't let himself be idle. He had to get his act together and fast.

Lily may think that she had everything under control. However, Lucifer knew the power and temptation of the Wicked Crown. He knew how hard it was to resist its caressing whispers. It had been hard to take the Wicked Crown off and even harder to stay away from it.

"Your majesty," a demoness stepped up to the side of the cot he laid on, her head bowed. He hadn't seen one of her kind in a long time, a barbas, known for their healing powers. She had the pale violet complexion of her kind, her almost white locks pulled up into a tight bun on her head between where her long-pointed ears stuck up on either side of her head. Her almost completely black irises glanced at him and then back at the ground when he met her gaze. "Can I get you anything?"

Shifting on the bed, his wings twinging with each movement, Lucifer shook his head. "No, I think I'm quite content for the moment. Are there many injured?" He glanced around the infirmary. There were curtains closing off each bed to give each of the injured or sick some form of privacy. Not that it helped with all of their superior hearing. Still, it was a nice touch that he had not thought of during his time of reign.

The demoness' gaze softened. "It is kind of you to worry for the others when you are injured yourself, your majesty. However, do not fret. There were not many that sustained such drastic injuries. You took on quite a lot of them yourself. There was hardly anything for the rest of the army to do."

Lucifer sank further into his bed, relief filling him. "I am glad to hear it. I'd hate for Hell to suffer more for my mistakes. Do not worry, I will fix things now that I am back."

When the demoness frowned, chewing on the dark violet color of her lips, Lucifer cocked his head to the side. "What is it?"

"It's nothing, your majesty. It's not for me to comment on."

Lucifer caught her wrist as she moved to leave. Her skin soft underneath his fingertips. "No please, speak freely. I would like to know the worries of my people."

The demoness paused, still unsure of whether or not she should speak. Lucifer dropped her wrist and sat up, hoping that it would encourage her to tell him what was on her mind.

"Well, your majesty," she added on quickly before continuing, "Many of us are concerned about what would become of you now that your daughter is here and with the..." she leaned forward and lowered her voice as if it were something taboo to say, "Wicked Crown." Straightening back up with her voice back to a normal pitch, she asked, "Are you still the ruler, or is she?" Her eyes widened and she waved her hands in front of her frantically.

"Not that we don't love your daughter. She saved us all today but she's not..."

As she trailed off, Lucifer nodded. "She's not me. I understand your concern. However, who is the primary ruler and who is not is not a major concern for me as of right now. Our biggest concern is making sure that our people are safe, and I believe both my daughter and myself want to see Hell thrive once more and those Utopian swine back where they belong. Don't you?" He offered her a genuine smile.

The demoness bobbed her head enthusiastically. "Yes, yes. Of course. Thank you for letting me know. It comforts me to know our kingdom is in good hands, whichever those are." She bowed at the waist before hurrying away. No doubt trying to save herself from embarrassment if the darkened color of her cheeks were anything to go by.

"That was quite diplomatic of you," a voice announced from the other side of him before the curtain was pulled open to reveal Astaroth.

"Why do you sound so surprised?" Lucifer shifted back onto the pillows, wishing he could pull his wings back in. They weren't healed enough to be put away though.

Astaroth smirked, his hands tucked

into his pockets as he stepped into the enclosed area. "I thought perhaps you had gotten feeble minded in your time locked away. I'm glad to see you are as quick witted as ever."

Lucifer arched his brow. "You are? Why don't I believe you?"

Chuckling, Astaroth stepped up to the bed. "Because your daughter is my mate, and I would do anything to make her happy. Even take Hell from her father. Though..." he trailed off and a seriousness filled his tone. "I don't think Lily is ready for anything of the sort and while I would do anything for her, I won't let her destroy herself either."

This made Lucifer sit up abruptly, throwing his legs over the side of the bed before he could think about the consequences of his actions. "What happened? Where is she?"

"Woah, woah," Astaroth held his hands up and ushered Lucifer back down to the bed. "No need to hurt yourself. She's fine. For now. I was able to get the Wicked Crown off of her but..." he sighed, gripping the back of his neck. "It's really got its claws into her. I wish I could do something to make it easier for her."

Lucifer shook his head. "She should never have taken the Wicked

Crown to begin with. She's not ready for the pull it has on its owner. If Lily is as strong willed as her parents, she will be able to hold her own for a little while but eventually the Wicked Crown will make her into a warped version of herself. One that doesn't care about family, friendship, or love."

He stared down at the ground trying not to think of his own time under the Wicked Crown's thrall. "All that will matter to her will be power and getting more of it." Lucifer paused and then looked up at him. "You said you got the Wicked Crown from her? How?"

Astaroth's frowned. "Not in a way I am proud of."

Lucifer inclined his head in under-standing. Sometimes we had to do horrible things for the ones we loved even if it was for their own good.

"I do have an idea of how to help her," Astaroth informed him.

Lucifer waited for him to continue.

"Distraction," he said simply. "If what she wants is to conquer and grab power, we need her to focus on some-thing that has nothing to do with those but could persuade her to think she is doing it to get power when in fact it's for another reason entirely."

"Perhaps I have been imprisoned

for too long." Lucifer leaned forward, his elbows on his knees. "I do not understand what you mean."

"Lilith."

The single name made Lucifer's palms sweat and his heart jerk in his chest. Lilith? How could his wife do anything for them? Of course, Lucifer wanted nothing more than to be with his wife again but finding her was a whole other challenge.

"I'm sorry to tell you but if the archangels were not able to find my wife again after she sequestered our daughter then I do not see how we would be able to?" Lucifer sighed and then chuckled fondly. "Lilith won't let herself be found if she does not want to be."

Astaroth simply stared down at him.

That was when it hit Lucifer. "You wouldn't be asking about Lilith if you didn't already know where she was would you?"

"I found your daughter when no one else in Utopia or Hell could, what makes you think I could not find your wife?" The smugness in Astaroth's voice made Lucifer want to hit the prince had the thought of seeing his wife again not overcome that annoyance.

"I could just kiss you." Lucifer burst up his arms open wide to envelope the demon before him in a hug but groaned and sat back down. "But I won't. Unfortunately, it seems that I will not be able to assist you in this just right now. Perhaps in a few hours."

Astaroth chuckled. "That's alright, old man. I think I've got this. However, I will need your assistance once we are ready to confront her." His lips ticked up a bit as he scratched the back of his head. "I'm afraid your wife might not believe me if I showed up on my own."

"She would if you brought Lily with you." There was no doubt in Lucifer's mind that Lilith would recognize their daughter just as he had. If Astaroth put Lily in front of her mother, there was nothing in the cosmos that would keep her away from her.

"Of course...but I do not think this is a mate thing." Astaroth continued. "I want to be Lily's everything. Her family, her life. And I will be but not until she has what she lost together again. And for that she needs you. She needs her father."

Lily

Sitting on the edge of her bed, Lily stared down at her hands. The hands that almost used her powers to hurt Roth. To hurt her mate.

Her hands opened and closed before her as if Lily were not quite sure they were real. How had it come to this? How had she let the Wicked Crown take over her so much?

When she'd first put the Wicked Crown on, she'd thought this was it. This was what she had been waiting for her whole life. However, now looking back...Lily had been a fool to give in so easily. Sure, they were in the middle of a battle. Roth had just been taken out and she alone couldn't have saved everyone without help. However, was the help she needed the Wicked Crown? If she had only waited a few more moments, Lily would have seen Raven and the others show up with the cavalry of sorts. And her father.

Oh, shit. Her father.

Lily dragged a hand through her violet hair and glanced over at the Wicked Crown. Such a small piece of metal to cause such heartache. Lily wished she'd never seen the stupid thing. Never heard its seductive whispers. Still, there was no taking it back now. She'd made her bed and now she had to lie in it.

Lily shifted on the bed, happy to be fully clothed once more. She was more than grateful to her mate for not only putting up with her but hunting down a servant to bring her something else to wear without making her look like a complete idiot.

Smoothing her hands over the skirt of the dark green gown, Lily sighed. The gown they'd brought her wasn't something she'd normally choose. It was far more frilly than practical. Though, she supposed she'd have been used to wearing gowns and the like if she had grown up in Hell as the princess and heir rather than on earth as the unwanted hell spawn.

Snorting, Lily realized how close to the truth her adoptive family had been.

"What would they think if they could see me now?" she murmured to herself.

"What would who think?"

Turning her head to the doorway, she smiled weakly at Raven. "The witches who raised me."

"Ah, those bitches. I wouldn't bother worrying about what they think." Raven walked into Lily's bedroom, a slight limping in her step that made Lily frown. "You never have to see them again."

"What's wrong? Did you get hurt during the fight? If so, you need to go to the infirmary to get checked out."

When her friend didn't answer right away, she stared at Raven until the Nephilim's cheeks pinked. Raven sank down on the bed slowly, wincing as she became fully seated. "No, I didn't get hurt during the battle. Just got a little carried away..."

Lily's brows furrowed. "Carried away? Doing what?"

Raven's face turned even redder, and she wouldn't meet Lily's gaze.

A lightbulb went off.

"Ah, you and Ash...it is Ash, right?" Lily cocked a brow, a mischievous grin overcoming her face.

Raven bumped her shoulder and scowled, "Of course it was Ash. And who knew a hellhound had such stamina. I could hardly keep up. I have a feeling I won't be walking right for days."

Lily giggled. "And that's a bad thing?"

"Hell no," Raven retorted and then quickly caught herself, "I mean, no it's not. Just never thought the beast had it in him."

Bobbing her head, Lily sighed. "I know what you mean. I'd never wanted to have sex with anyone until Roth and now I can't seem to get enough of him. It's just so...so..." she fought for the word to describe her need for him.

"Addictive?"

"Yes," Lily grinned at Raven. "Exactly. It's like the more I get of him the more I want. You'd think I'd be tired of him by now, even when he..." Lily trailed off not wanting to talk about her failure.

Raven placed her hand on Lily's. "It's okay. Roth told me everything. That's actually why I came by. To check on you. Are you okay?" Her eyes shifted from Lily to the Wicked Crown. "I mean, really? Not just some bs you fed your mate to keep him off your back."

Lily swallowed and bobbed her head. "Yeah, no. Fuck. I don't know. It's all so confusing. What I think is my thoughts aren't my thoughts and what I felt while wearing the Wicked Crown," she looked away from the shiny black metal while she remembered, "I'm not sure I can keep myself from hurting my loved ones while wearing it. All it wants is power and more power. It doesn't care who it destroys in the process, even me."

Raven squeezed her hand. "Then we'll have to be here to make sure that doesn't happen."

Shaking her head violently, Lily shoved away from Raven and paced the room. "You don't understand. I can feel it," Lily grabbed the material of her dress above her heart, "in here. Clawing and biting at me. Just waiting for a moment of weakness for me to pick it up again. Even now, there's a part of me that wants to hurt Roth for taking it away from me."

"And yet, you are sitting here next to it and haven't put it on," Raven pointed out from her seat on the bed. "I think that's more important than what you are thinking or feeling. Your actions define you, not what you want to do." Raven smirked. "I want to punch out every single one of those harpy bitches at the school and yet I didn't. Why?"

Lily huffed a laugh. "Because you would get in trouble."

"No," Raven narrowed her eyes at her. "Because my purpose there was far greater than my desire to beat up a bunch of prissy human girls." Raven stood and walked over to her, taking her hands. "If I had blown my cover, I would never have found you and I think that's worth so much more than the momentary satisfaction I would get from seeing Nathalie flail about over a broken nose."

They laughed together.

"Yeah, I could see that," Lily said, her eyes drifting to the Wicked Crown as she licked her lips to ask, "Do you really think I can do it? Use the power and not be consumed by it?"

"Fuck yeah! You're Lily Star Morgan and you can do anything." Raven wrapped an arm around her shoulders and led her toward the door. "Now, let's go find the guys and get something to eat. I'm starving."

Lily snorted. "Yeah, after all those calories you burned I would be too." When they got to the bedroom door, Lily paused, unable to go any further. "Do you think the Wicked Crown will be alright in here? With no one to guard it?"

Raven arched her brow. "It wasn't guarded before you took it was it?"

Lily shook her head. "No, it was just

sitting there in a big room all by itself. The door wasn't even locked."

"Then I wouldn't worry about it." Raven patted her shoulder. "I don't think anyone wants that thing any more than you do."

That was the problem though. Lily did want it. More than she wanted anything else in her entire life. She only hoped she was strong enough to fight back the want before it ripped everything she held dear from her grasp.

Roth

Swirling the dark amber liquid around in his glass, Roth tried to keep his thoughts light so as not to darken the mood of the meal. Sadly, the more he thought about what was ahead of them the harder it was to keep the shadows from creeping in.

"Oh yes, food!" Ash cried out and rushed the table, eating off his plate before he even sat down.

Roth's lips twitched. There was more than one reason he kept the hellhound around. Not only was he loyal to a fault but Roth could always rely on Ash to bring light into the room.

"It would be a miracle if any of the food found its way to your plate before it hits your stomach, Ash." Roth eyed the hellhound, arching a brow. "Wear yourself out?"

Ash grinned through a mouthful of food. "That obvious?"

Shrugging a shoulder, Roth sat his glass down on the table before him. "It is to me. Please, you reek of the Nephilim." His nose wrinkled in protest.

Eyes narrowed, Ash pointed a chicken leg at Roth. "Hey, that's my mate you're talking about. You don't hear me complaining about how almost every room in your wing smells of sex, now do you?"

Roth smirked. "That's my right as Duke of Hell and mate to the heir of Hell."

"Queen, you mean," Ash corrected him, pulling apart a piece of bread. "Don't let her hear you say otherwise. Who knows what she'll do with that thing on her head now."

"I wouldn't worry too much about that. I have taken care of it," Roth told Ash with a wry smile.

Raven walked in at that moment with Lily close behind her. She grabbed a grape off the table and popped it into her mouth before plopping herself down on a chair beside Ash, throwing her feet up on the edge of the table and asked, "Taken care of what?"

Lily made a more quiet entrance,

pulling her chair out beside Roth so slow that it didn't make a sound before sitting down. The utter despair on her face made his heart ache. She avoided anyone's gaze, her eyes down on her plate as she chewed on her lower lip.

"Lily." Roth reached out his hand and offered it to Lily. For a moment, he didn't think she would take it. Then she brought her hand up from her lap and gently laid her hand in his before lifting her gaze from her plate to meet Roth's. What he saw there broke his heart.

Ash broke the tension. "Hey, Lil," he gave her a lopsided grin, jerking his chin toward her head. "I see you're missing an...uh...accessory there."

Lily winced.

Roth squeezed Lily's hand in a comforting gesture while shooting Ash a glare. The hellhound wasn't affected by his look and continued to chat away as if he hadn't brought up the elephant in the room.

"You know, for a second there I thought we were gonna lose." Ash grabbed his glass and chugged half of it before slamming it down on the table with a satisfied breath. "Then you come blasting out of the castle, new wings and everything. I swore I almost fainted at the sight. By the way..." Ash cocked his head to the side. "Where are your wings? Most newbies can't get them back in the first few days. So, they go walking around with them sticking out, getting stuck in doorways, knocking over people. It's pretty hilarious actually." He chuckled to himself not noticing the tension in Lily's shoulders had gotten tighter.

"Ash," Raven grabbed her mate's arm, her eyes narrowing. "Shut up."

"What?" Ash's brows furrowed as he looked at Raven and then to Roth and Lily. "What's the problem? The Wicked Crown is off. We won the fight. We should be celebrating, not acting like someone died." Ash chuckled and then stopped midway with a frown. "Wait, did someone die?"

"No, you insensitive prick," Raven smacked him over the back of the head with a scowl. "But read the room. Lily doesn't want to talk about it."

Ash glanced away from his mate to Lily, finally noticing how upset she was with all his chatter. Face falling, Ash hurried out, "Ah, Lil, I'm sorry. I didn't mean anything by it. You really did look cool. And you saved us all. Don't let that overshadow anything that piece of metal made you do-" Lily shoved her chair back and stood from the table, walking out the door. Ash gaped after her, asking Raven, "What did I say?"

Roth followed Lily, catching up to her in the hallway. He took her by the hand, causing her to pause.

Lily turned slightly toward him, keeping her face turned away. "I can't do this. I can't sit in there and pretend like I didn't almost…"

Stepping closer to her, Roth reached out and turned her face toward him, sweeping his thumb under her eyes to catch her tears. "The important thing is that you didn't. I won't lie to you and pretend like this won't be hard. Your father said -"

Lily's face changed into a snarl. "My father can go back to the prison he hid in for the last millennia."

Roth sighed and continued, "Your father said that the Wicked Crown would still have some influence over you even if you've taken it off. It will take time to feel like your normal self again."

Lily shook her head and stepped back from him, wrapping her arms around herself. "You don't understand, Roth." She licked her lips and swallowed her eyes staring down at the ground. "I want it. It's gnawing at me right now not to have it and while I do feel bad about almost blasting you, it doesn't take away the fact that all I want to do right now is run back to my room and put the damn thing back on my head." Finally, she turned her gaze back to him, a desperate longing in her eyes that had nothing to do with him and everything to do with the Wicked Crown. Her voice broke as she said, "I want it more than I want to breathe, Roth. I've never felt that way about anything, not even you."

Gathering her up into his arms, Roth stroked her hair as he murmured softly in her ear. "I know, baby. I know. And we're going to be here helping you through it. You just have to let us in."

Burying her face in his chest, Lily mumbled, "But what if I try to hurt you again?"

Roth chuckled a dark sound that reverberated through his chest. "Then I guess I should go make nice with the Wicked Crown. Perhaps then it will make sure to spare me if I anger it again."

Lily lifted her head and gave him an impatient look. "That's not what I mean and you know it. The Wicked Crown doesn't give a fuck about you or anyone else. It just wants power and destruction. Two things you can't give it."

"Well," Roth stroked a hand over

her hair and kissed her temple. "I better make myself useful so it doesn't decide I'm better off dead."

Arching a brow, Lily asked, "How are you going to do that?"

Roth cupped her face with his hands and brought his lips to hers in a gentle kiss. Withdrawing, he announced, "By giving you the one thing you've wanted your whole life."

Lily stared up at him, confusion wrinkling her brow.

"A family."

Ash

❧❀☙

Once Lily and Roth were out of the room, Raven shoved him hard enough that he fell out of his chair. "Hey! What was that for?" Ash asked from the ground.

Raven sighed and shook her head. "How I'm in love with you, I have no idea."

Ash grinned at her as he climbed back into his seat, leaning toward her. "You're in love with me, huh?"

Scowling, Raven tugged on his hair sharply. "Don't make a big deal of it or I'll cut off your favorite appendage."

"As I recall from earlier," Ash shifted closer to her, sliding his fingers up and down her thigh over her leggings. "It's your favorite appendage too."

Chewing her food thoughtfully, Raven gave him a sideways look. "What are we going to do?"

"Well, I have a few ideas," Ash smirked, shifting his chair even closer to hers, his cock becoming hard beneath his pants.

Rolling her eyes at him, Raven picked at her food. "I mean about Lily. And I'm not having sex with you in here. Anyone could walk in."

"Oh come on, that's half the fun," Ash murmured in her ear, placing an open mouth kiss on her neck where he knew she liked.

Raven swallowed hard, her arousal spiking briefly before her eyes turned away from him and to the doorway. "Father, I didn't know you were still here."

Ash sighed and slinked back to his own chair at a respectable distance while the archangel watched him curiously. "Michael," he bobbed his head in greeting.

The archangel walked into the room like he owned the place, taking up a seat at the other end of the table. He sat down and began to serve himself, his eyes flickering to Raven and Ash every few moments. When he was settled he locked his eyes on his daughter. "So tell me, what are your intentions with my daughter, hound?"

Ash choked on the drink he was in the middle of swallowing. "Excuse me?"

"Father," Raven bit out, grabbing a hold of Ash's hand. "That's out of line."

Michael shot a look at his daughter, arching a brow before returning his laser gaze on Ash. "I simply want to make sure my heir is in good hands."

"Believe me," Raven squeezed his hand in hers. "I'm in the best hands in all of the Underworld. And do you really think you can have a say in my life now? After all these years? I think that's a bit pointless don't you think?"

Michael inclined his head. "Perhaps, but I wish to know you better and to do that I must know the one you will link yourself to for the rest of your life. I will not have my daughter mistreated, do you hear me beast?"

"Stop calling him that," Raven snapped. "He has a name."

Michael slid his eyes over to Ash and drawled out, "Yes, Ash, is it? What kind of name is that?"

Used to people treating him like trash all of his life for who he was and where he came from, Ash shrugged a shoulder not at all bothered by the archangel's words. "You'd have to ask my parents. I didn't pick it."

"And where are they?" Michael picked up his glass and held it between both hands, waiting for the answer to his question.

Ash stabbed his fork into a green bean, he bit into the end of it. "No idea." He replied through bites. "They're dead as far as I know."

"That is...unfortunate," Michael drew out, swirling the liquid in his glass with a hum. "And where do you plan to live with my daughter after the issues with Utopia are done?"

This had Ash sitting up and paying attention. His eyes found Raven's question in his eyes.

"Uh, we haven't really discussed that yet," Raven answered for them, narrowing her eyes on her father. "And honestly it's none of your business what we decide to do."

"Now, now, retract your claws, daughter." Michael sat his glass down on the table and shifted in his seat, picking up his silverware. "I simply wish to know that my daughter is safe and taken care of."

"You mean, like you have my whole life?" Raven pointed out with a knowing look.

Ash couldn't help the little smile

that crept up his face at her words, so he covered it by taking a drink from his glass. He didn't want to get on the bad side of the archangel but he also wasn't going to let the man walk all over him either. He didn't have a relationship with his parents but Ash felt that though Raven protested against having a relationship with her father, he didn't want to stand in the way of that.

"Raven," Ash glanced at her and then to her father. "He's just trying to make up for lost time. I wouldn't want to cause any rift between you, besides, if we have pups I'd want them to know their grandfather." Ash winked at Michael, who looked as if he had swallowed something sour.

"Pups?" Raven squeaked.

Ash turned his gaze toward his mate. "Well, I'm not talking about now, but sometime in the future we may decide that we want to have a litter and wouldn't it be nice if they knew your father? I mean, he could babysit and everything, really making up for lost time."

Michael cleared his throat and pushed away from the table. "Yes, well, while that is something to think about, I'm sure that is in the far, far future. I think I will go check up on my brother." He cleared his throat again. "Yes, exactly."

Once the archangel left the room, Ash burst into laughter, throwing his head back until he couldn't breathe from laughing so hard.

"Haha, very funny," Raven drew out dryly and then a worried look pinched her face. "You don't really mean a whole litter, do you?"

Ash saddled up next to her and brushed a piece of her black hair behind her ear before kissing her on the cheek. "That highly depends on you but I will have all the pups you want and then some."

"What if I don't want any?" Raven pointed out with a wrinkle of her nose.

Shrugging a shoulder, Ash picked up her hand and kissed it. "Then we'll spend the rest of our lives fucking on every world and continent." He licked along the length of one of her fingers before nipping at the tip.

Raven giggled and wiggled her hand out of his grasp. "Alright, alright. Don't go planning our itinerary now. We have to get out of this mess first."

"Oh, yeah." Ash frowned and glanced at the door that Lily and Roth had exited. "The Wicked Crown."

"No, that asshole Gabriel," Raven reminded him. "I spent the last few years with him and I know him. He's not going to just go off and leave us alone. I'm sure he's made his plans to come back and strike at us tenfold."

Ash hummed. "Well, we'll just have to make sure that we're ready for him."

Lucifer

His shoulder was on fire as Lucifer shrugged into his shirt. That barbas was a lot more stubborn than he had remembered. Lucifer wanted to be out of the infirmary the same day he went into it but the demoness had insisted that Lucifer stay there until the next day.

Now while trying to get dressed, Lucifer was seeing what the demoness meant. He had spent far too long locked away and content to play chess with any angel that would bother to visit him than keep in shape. He might be immortal but he could still die and with how much Lucifer hurt right then, he felt as if he might at any moment.

"This is just pathetic," a familiar voice said from the doorway of Lucifer's new guest room.

Snorting, Lucifer fastened each button of his shirt with painful precision. "Laugh it up now, you'll never get another chance, brother."

Michael stepped into Lucifer's bedroom with a chuckle. "I highly doubt that. Your daughter is one fiery creature and I do not think any of us will be able to get back to normal until she has brought down Gabriel."

Lifting his head, Lucifer's gaze hardened. "I cannot say that I blame her. I would like a word or two with our siblings as well." Straightening the cuffs of his shirt, he turned to his brother. "How are things going with your own offspring?"

Michael made a face.

"That badly, huh?" Lucifer chuckled.

Sighing, Michael strolled over to the window and stared out of it as he spoke, "I feel as if you had the right idea binding your child to a mate at birth."

Throwing his head back and laughing, Lucifer shook his head. "Believe me, it's not all it's cracked up to be. Though, I have to say Astaroth is a far deal different than a hellhound."

Michael huffed over his shoulder. "That is an understatement. It is hard to believe that...that mutt is mated to my daughter. How does one deal with such a thing?"

Lucifer shrugged. "It's not your choice. As much as we would like to, we cannot control our children's lives and the more we try, the more they will rebel against us."

"You would know," Michael smirked at him.

"Yes, well," Lucifer scratched the back of his head with a genuine smile. "The heart wants what it wants."

"I heard from Astaroth you will be setting out to find her soon."

"Lilith?" Lucifer bobbed his head. "Yes. That is the plan."

"Are you nervous?" Michael walked over to him, his eyes boring into him. "It has been a long time since you've seen each other."

Lucifer winced. "I am far less worried about myself and more about how Lily will react to her mother. She hasn't exactly embraced me with open arms, or you know, anything other than disdain. I do not wish the same for her mother."

Michael frowned. "You do know some of that was the Wicked Crown talking?"

"I am well aware of what kind of hold the Wicked Crown has on its wearer. I did wear it for more than a century." Lucifer adjusted his collar and stalked toward the door. "I am also aware that it does not make you say things you do not already feel in your heart. My daughter has no love for me. However, I plan to change that. First with reuniting her with her mother and then I will figure out the rest as I go."

Lucifer left Michael behind in his room to ponder what he had said. There were many things he would come to his brother for advice on but his daughter wasn't one of them. It was common knowledge that archangels were not the best of parents. Probably because they didn't exactly have the best father figure themselves. Trying to figure out how to be a good parent wasn't something they knew how to do. Lucifer was trying though. He would not be like his father. Distant and only deeming them worthy of his presence when he had a command for them to carry out.

Walking down the hallway to the front of the palace, Lucifer wondered how Astaroth had figured out where his wife was located. If Lilith did not want to be found, there was no one on this planet or the next that could find her. Not even Lucifer.

While he had told Michael that he

didn't worry about meeting Lilith again, that wasn't exactly true. Lucifer hadn't seen his wife in years and the thought of seeing her energized and terrified him at the same time. He could not wait to have his lovely mate back into his arms and yet he feared all the time apart might have made her less inclined to care for him.

Had she found someone else during his imprisonment? He wouldn't blame her. Lilith was a gorgeous creature worth all the love and pleasure anyone who was lucky enough to come into her beautiful gaze could give her. Lucifer hoped that he was able to rekindle the love they once had.

"What the fuck is he doing here?" Lily snarled in Lucifer's direction as he approached her and Astaroth.

"So glad to see you too daughter," Lucifer dryly greeted, stopping before them. Turning his gaze to the duke, he nodded, "Astaroth."

"Lucifer," Astaroth inclined his head in return. Astaroth turned to Lily and placed a hand on her waist. "Your father is going to help us find your mother."

Lily turned her scowl to her mate. "My mother? Why do we need to find her?"

Astaroth pursed his lips and then

leaned his head down to press his forehead to hers. "For you, my mate. As well as for your father and the people. They need to see their leaders rejoined so that we can rebuild the Underworld to its former glory. That is what you want, isn't it?" He stroked his thumb across her cheek and along her jawline. "To be unstoppable?"

Lily leaned into his touch with a sigh, her eyes sliding over to Lucifer with a reluctant huff. "Fine. But don't blame me if I accidentally push him in front of a bus."

Lucifer arched his brow. "I'll make sure to watch my back then."

Giving him a shit eating grin, Lily pushed away from Astaroth and said, "I'd watch a whole of a hell more than that, your majesty."

Ash

With the royal family otherwise occupied, Ash had one thing on his mind.

His mate.

And more precisely, getting his dick and every other part of himself on her as often as he could.

Following her flowery scent down the hallway, Ash felt his blood heating and churning. There was nothing more invigorating than the hunt and while he and Raven had already consummated their relationship, just the action of hunting her down was almost better than any kind of foreplay.

Almost.

"Raven, where are you?" Ash murmured to himself in a sing-song voice. "I have something to give you that I think you're going to like. Or at least I will." Ash smirked and pushed open the door to the training room where Raven's scent was strongest.

When he stepped into an empty room, Ash frowned, his brows furrowed tightly together. "Well, damn. Where is she?"

Ash sniffed around the room briefly, finding remnants of his mate's scent and even more heavily on a discarded towel. He brought the towel up to his face and inhaled deeply, the smell of it stirred his blood and his cock with need.

Sighing as he adjusted himself with one hand, Ash tossed the towel aside. "She was just here. Where could she have gone?"

Ash started for the door. A breeze stopped him. Turning back to the room, Ash lifted his head toward the roof where a large opening that he'd never seen before laid. Sniffing the air, Ash growled.

Of course, Raven had taken to the sky. Now it'd take him hours to find her with the wind throwing her scent about the way it was.

Reluctantly, Ash left the training room and made his way down the hall-way. Maybe he'd get lucky and Raven had already gone back to her room? With it on the other side of the building he wouldn't sense it from here. She could have come in from her balcony and he'd have never known.

Determined to find her himself, Ash stalked toward the guest rooms. He, himself, had one in that part of the castle so if anything he could take a nap while he waited for Raven to return. Unfortunately, with his luck, Raven's angelic cock blocking father would be there too and then he'd never get a moment alone with his mate.

On his way through the hallways a group of frantic looking demonesses were whispering to each other. The moment they saw Ash they quieted and all but one rushed away, the others tossing worried and pitying looks to the one left behind.

"What is it?" Ash inquired, not liking the way the others had made a mad dash for it.

The demoness rubbed her hands together, her tail moving back and forth anxiously. Her large black eyes kept glancing back at the door behind her.

"What's going on?" Ash crossed his arms over his chest and stared down the demoness.

"I...I...really should speak to her majesty about it."

That's when Ash realized the door

they were in front of belonged to Lily. His frown deepening, Ash pushed past the demoness and reached for the door handle. The demoness quickly tried to speak as he walked into the room.

"We don't even know if it is really missing and we didn't want to cause a commotion about it until we were sure."

Ash scanned the room searching for what was out of place. "What's missing?"

The demoness moved around him until she was by the bed, her hand on her face pleading for him to listen to her. "That's just it. It may not be missing. We don't know. Since her majesty and the king are the only ones who can touch it, we thought perhaps they moved it back to the vault."

At her words, Ash froze. His gaze immediately went to the pillow on the side table of Lily's bed where he knew held the Wicked Crown. That pillow was empty.

"Did someone move it?" The demoness asked, her voice shaking.

Ash's gaze hardened, his jaw clenched tight. "No, no they didn't." Ash turned abruptly on his heel and stalked out of the room. His destination the same. However, now all his thoughts were on something else.

Something terrible that might ruin them all.

It didn't take him long to cross the castle and arrive at Raven's bedroom door. Ash paused in front of the door unsure if he should knock or not. Thinking to play it safe, Ash knocked on the door twice.

"Come on in, Ash." Raven's voice called from inside the room. The very sound of his mate's voice calmed the anxiety rushing through his body.

Tentatively, Ash opened the door and walked in. His nose zeroed in on where his mate stood clad in nothing but a towel, her hair wet and dangling around her face. For a millisecond, Ash's thoughts turned back to the original reason he had been searching for her and he swallowed his words.

"Were you looking for me?" Raven smirked and sashayed over to him, letting the towel slip ever so slightly as she moved, teasing him with each agonizing inch it bared of her until it was almost to the ground. "Looks like you found me."

"Yeah..." Ash drew out slowly as his eyes followed that towel's path. All the blood in his body rushed to his cock and the reason he had come went completely out the window.

Raven placed her hands on his

chest, stroking a hand up and down it while she pressed that delectable body of hers up against him. "You know, I was hoping to run into you."

"Oh yeah?" Ash asked distractedly, his hands falling to her bare hips. "Did you miss me?"

Leaning in close, Raven brushed her lips against Ash's and murmured, "Oh yes, most definitely, especially a certain part of you." Her hand suddenly cupped his erection and Ash let out a long groan, his eyes rolling up into his head. "You know with Lily and the others gone I thought we could spend this time getting to know each other better..." she stroked him up and down through his pants, making Ash pant and moan.

Ash pushed back the pleasure of having his mate touch him as her words came through clear. Lily and the others. The Wicked Crown. Right. That was what he came for. Shit. He never had much self-control and now he would have to extort every bit of it right then.

"I can't." Ash shifted away from Raven's touch, taking a step back and turning his gaze to the side so as not to be tempted.

"What do you mean you can't?" Raven prodded, stepping toward him once more. "It seemed very well like you can."

Ash shook his head and turned his gaze back to her, making sure to keep his eyes locked on hers. "I mean we can't. Not right now. As much as it pains me to say it, there's something else more important right now." Unable to stop himself, Ash's gaze slid down his mate's body one more time and he let out a whimper before turning his back on her. "Please put some clothes on because this is hard enough as it is."

"Okay..." Raven drew out and there was a shuffle behind him before she stated, "There. I'm decent. You can look now and explain to me what's so important you had to hurt a girl's pride like that."

Ash's heart sank as he slowly turned around, making sure Raven was completely clothed before turning completely. With a sigh of disappointment, Ash reluctantly faced his mate. "Thank you and I promise I will make it up to you...at length." He let her see all his desire in his eyes before continuing, "We have a problem."

"I gathered as much when you said no to sex." Raven crossed her arms under her chest, pushing her ample breasts up to tease the neckline of her tank top. "What's the problem?"

Shaking his head to clear it, Ash forced his eyes back to her face. "The Wicked Crown is gone."

"Shit." Raven dropped her arms, pulling her lip between her teeth to gnaw on it. "You don't think?"

"Lily took it with her when they went to find Lilith?" Ash finished for her with a scowl. "Yes, I do."

"We should call Ash." Raven stalked over to her bed and grabbed her cell phone. Fingers posed over the screen, Raven scowled, "Crap, we can't. No service in Hell."

Ash shrugged and sauntered over to her. "Well, what should we do? Go after them? We could probably catch up to them if we hurry."

Raven stared down at her phone and sighed. "No, we can't. We have to go with Michael soon, remember? Besides," Raven added on, "it'll be fine. What trouble could Lily get into with Lucifer and Roth there?" She paused for a second and then bobbed her head as if trying to convince herself. "Yeah. Yeah. It'll be okay. It'll be fine. Won't it?"

Lily

This was the stupidest idea in the world. The universe. Why did Roth think that they needed Lucifer to come with them to find her mother? How did he even know where her mother was? Lily had spent a number of her younger years trying to find her mother and had been unsuccessful. What made Roth so confident he knew where she was?

"Stop brooding," Roth murmured to her, wrapping an arm around her waist to drag her close to his side. "You're getting wrinkles between your brows."

Lily scowled, adjusting her bag on her shoulder. "I'm not brooding."

"Pouting then," Roth corrected, darting a look behind him at their shadow. "He's trying to be there for you and you're hardly putting in any effort."

Peeking over her shoulder, Lily narrowed her eyes at the archangel. "I don't know why you think I need to play nice with him. It's not like he put any effort into finding me all this time. From what Raven said, he sat in luxury playing chess for the last few hundred years."

"He was keeping you safe. You know that and I thought you were putting those thoughts behind you? The Wicked Crown is all the way back in Hell, I'd have thought the distance would be enough to help you see clearer."

Lily forced herself not to tense up at the mention of the Wicked Crown. "You're right. I'll try harder to get along with him. I'm not calling him Dad though."

Roth chuckled and kissed her on top of the head. "I wouldn't expect you to do anything you're not comfortable with."

"Like you could," Lily teased, leaning into his embrace. "Where are we going anyway?" Lily's gaze scanned around them, eyes narrowing as she realized they were in a familiar area. "Wait a second...this is...that can't be right." She pushed away from Roth and stopped in front of him. "This is the way to my school."

Roth met her gaze and calmly stated, "It is indeed," before he continued walking past her.

Lily hurried to catch up, not sparing Lucifer a glance and grabbed Roth's arm. "Hey, don't just say that and walk away. Are you telling me my mother has been this close to me this whole time and didn't reach out to me?"

Lucifer's voice came from behind them. "The same reason I've spent the last few thousand years twiddling my thumbs as you say...to keep you safe."

Lily hummed, trying to keep herself from saying something unkind. The weight of Lucifer's words weighed heavily on her and all she could think about was why was everything more important than actually being there for her? She'd have rather been dead than grow up without a family that loved her. The witches were hardly what Lily would call a loving family. Even though there were dozens of them, Lily felt more alone with them than by herself.

"It's just right up here." Roth pointed to an apartment complex on the corner.

The same exact apartment complex Lily had lived in before. Rage gnawed at Lily's heart. Her fingers clenched and unclenched around the strap of her purse. Her footsteps slowed and it seemed as if time had stopped all around her and each step was harder than the last.

Could she really deal with another parent showing up? Did she want to? No. Not really. Lily wasn't a coward though. If she fled out of fear, she'd never forgive herself. She'd imagined this day before. The day she'd finally see her mom again. And this was nothing like she had expected. There was no crying embrace. There was probably not going to be any long talks into the night about what we'd both been doing the last decade or so of her life. Lily certainly didn't expect any of that to happen with her mate and father in tow. Not with all of heaven breathing down their necks and the Wicked Crown in her purse.

"Lily?" Roth paused at the end of the street, peering back at her. "What's wrong?"

Lucifer stopped at her side and waved Roth off. "Go on ahead. We'll be there in a moment."

Brows raised, Lily stared at Lucifer for a moment wondering what he wanted. Roth lingered waiting for her to tell him it was alright. Lily sighed. "It's fine. Go ahead."

Roth hesitated for a moment before nodding. He stepped into the building and Lily turned back to Lucifer. "What do you want?"

Lucifer reached out to touch her. Lily stiffened and Lucifer withdrew his hand instead dragging it through his hair. "Look, I know we have not started off on the right foot and you have every right to be angry with me and your mother. But put yourself in our shoes." Lucifer continued while Lily clenched her jaw tightly. Every word he said only made the anger inside of Lily rise higher and higher inside of her. "We didn't want to leave you. We just wanted to protect you. To keep you away from those assholes in Utopia who wanted to hurt you."

"But you hurt me." Lily pointed out. "You left me and mom all alone. And then she gave me away to the witches and I never saw her again. Tell me how that's not the same thing? I would liter-ally rather be fighting for my life with my parents than facing it alive and alone." Lily straightened and took a step back from Lucifer. "But it doesn't matter anymore. I have Roth now. I don't need you."

The look on Lucifer's face was not

the one Lily expected. She had been aiming to hurt him and instead he looked at her with such pity and disappointment that the Wicked Crown gripped at her heart harder. You don't need them. Look how they feel about you. They don't want you either.

"Look, can we do this later." Lily huffed and crossed her arms. "Go tell Roth, I'll be there in a minute. I just need...I need a minute to prepare."

Lucifer watched her for a moment before inclining his head slowly. He turned on his heel and walked away. Lily waited until he was out of sight before bolting down the street. She had to get the fuck out of there.

Raven

❧

"I really think we should go find Lily and them." Raven murmured to Ash behind her dad's back as they walked through the woods off the edge of the main Utopia compound. "There's no telling what she's going to do with that crown influencing her."

"Shhh," Ash wrapped an arm around her shoulders and pulled her closer to him. "It'll be fine. I promise. What's she going to do? Run off? Roth and Lucifer wouldn't let that happen. They know how sensitive she is right now. Leaving her alone would be madness."

"Yeah, you're right." Raven sighed and moved away from Ash. "There's no way they'd let her out of their sight." To Michael she said, "Are you sure you know where you're going? This doesn't look right."

Michael paused and said over his shoulder, "If you had spent more time in Utopia than on Earth then you would know this is precisely the correct way to the hidden entrance into the compound."

Raven crossed her arms and glared at the back of his head. "And if you had cared one ounce about what I did growing up then maybe I would have spent more time here rather than on Earth."

Ash grabbed her hand and gave it a squeeze. "Come on now, let's focus on the task at hand. Finding out what that twat waffle, Gabriel is up to."

Holding onto Ash's hand tightly, Raven grunted, "Still not sure we're going the right way."

We walked through a bunch of trees until Michael came to an abrupt stop. "We're here."

"Fucking finally," Raven breathed, pushing up beside Michael. "What's this?" She frowned at the hole in the ground.

"Our way in," Michael explained, pushing his wings in until they faded away and stepped up to the hole.

"Uh...you've got to be kidding me." Raven stepped back from the hole, her stomach in her throat. "I'm not going down there."

Michael paused at the edge and arched a brow at her. "I never figured you for one to be afraid of anything?"

Raven scowled but didn't move any closer to the hole. "I'm not afraid. I Just don't understand why we have to go into that dank dark hole. Why do you even have a hole like that? Everything else here is bright and shiny. Why can't you have a secret passageway that's lit up too?"

Michael arched a brow at her. "Then it wouldn't be a secret passageway. Besides, it is not that dark." He took one step forward and dropped into the hole.

Raven leaned forward listening for the sound of his drop to the ground. When there was no following thump, Raven took a tentative step forward and called out, "Michael? Are you okay?" He didn't answer. Panic gripped Raven. "Michael? Dad? Dad, where are you? Hold on, I'm coming." She squatted down at the hole until she sat on the ground with her feet dangling in the hole. She glanced up at Ash. "What are you just standing there for? Come on, he might be hurt!"

Ash sighed and threw his hands up. "Alright."

Taking a deep breath, Raven closed her eyes and shoved herself off the side and into the darkness below...and landed barely six feet down. Raven frowned up at the hole above and saw Ash's feet coming over. She stepped out of the way and searched around the tunnel that was actually lined with dim lights until she found her father standing at the other end of the tunnel fiddling with something on the stone wall.

"Come along now," Michael called to them. "We don't want to linger here."

Raven blew out a long breath and shook her head. At least, Michael hadn't heard her freaking out. That was a blessing.

A slight bit of wind hit her back signaling Ash's descent. He found her right away and then saw Michael ahead. "Would you look at that? He's fine. See," He gripped her shoulders and massaged them slightly. "No need to worry."

"I wasn't," Raven sniffed and brushed his hands off her shoulders. "I was just concerned."

"Sure, you were," Ash drew out with a slight chuckle that earned him a glare from Raven. He picked up her hand and kissed it with a small smile. "Come on, my mate. Let's get this over with and then we can go home and we can celebrate the fact that your father is still alive...naked."

Raven's nose wrinkled. "You are a weird one."

"You love me anyway," Ash shot back with a smirk.

Shaking her head once more, Raven followed him down the tunnel. They came up behind Michael just as he got the door to click open. There was some kind of complex mechanism that required him to move each piece in a specific order before the door would unlock. Seemed more like something in a human movie than an angel thing.

"So where exactly does this tunnel come out at?" Ash asked Michael as they ducked into the next tunnel which was more like a hallway in one of the pristine white castles than an underground pathway. Big bright lights filled the room with so much light that it almost hurt to keep her eyes open.

Michael didn't stop as he answered, "Underneath my home. We can get more information once we arrive."

"But won't Gabriel be waiting for you to show up at home?" Ash inquired, holding Raven's hand more tightly.

Glancing over his shoulder,

Michael eyed the two of them. "Even if he was, there is nothing he can do. His crusade to capture the heir was never mine. We are both on the same level. He has no more power over me than I have over him."

Raven frowned. "Then why can't you just go to God and ask him to stop?"

Michael paused and turned around suddenly. "If you think God cares about what his underlings do then you are sorely overestimating his desire to be in the loop of the day-to-day workings of our world. He is more of a hands-off type of leader."

Ash snorted. "And you call us the evil ones."

"Either way," Michael continued, turning back to the tunnel, "The only ones who would care what I was doing are here in the tunnel. Even my fellow archangels have better things to do. They have their own assignments."

"But I thought everyone was looking for Lily?" Raven hurried forward. "That was what this whole thing was about. Finding Lily, stopping Lucifer from taking over Utopia..."

Michael huffed a laugh. "If you think my brother cares anything about Utopia you really don't know him. He only wants to live in his own little world with Lilith and now Lily. I can clearly see now that Gabriel and the others had been wrong about thinking our brother had greater ambitions."

"It could have just been the Wicked Crown talking at the time," Ash pointed out, coming up behind them. "Maybe he did want to take over Utopia because of the Wicked Crown and once he got it away from him, he stopped?"

Raven stopped in her tracks and slowly turned to Ash. "You don't think that Lily will do the same, do you?"

Ash shrugged a shoulder. "Maybe. I wouldn't put it past her."

"Hold on," Michael interrupted. "I thought Roth got the Wicked Crown away from Lily?"

Ash and Raven exchanged a look and Raven grimaced. "Yeah...about that..."

Roth

❧❧❧

Standing in the entryway of the apartment building, Roth waited for Lucifer and Lily to appear. He knew that Lily would be upset about her mother being so close to her and Roth wished there was some way to break the news gently. However, with everything going on and the Wicked Crown tempting her at every turn, Roth had to do something that would keep her mind off of it. Now if only Lucifer could not trigger her into taking off.

After a few minutes passed, Roth began to worry. He stepped toward the door, intent on finding them only for Lucifer to appear a moment later. "There you are, I was beginning to wonder." Roth frowned as he realized Lucifer had come in alone. "Where's Lily?"

Lucifer pushed past Roth and headed for the stairs. "She needed a moment to collect herself."

Roth's brows furrowed together. A moment to collect herself...well he supposed that made sense after whatever Lucifer had said to her but he wasn't sure leaving her on her own was the best idea.

"How did she seem when you left her?" Roth asked, catching up to Lucifer on the stairs. "Was she upset? Anxious?"

Lucifer paused on the stairs, his expression stoic with thought. "I'd have to say that she seemed alright. Perhaps a little tense but that could only be expected with all that's happened."

"Shit," Roth scowled and darted back down the stairs.

"What's wrong?" Lucifer called after him and then, "Why are you so worried?" as Lucifer chased after him. "Lily did not seem at all like she might take off on her own."

Roth scoffed. "Shows how much you know your daughter. She's had to train herself not to be overwhelmed by her emotions to keep her powers in check. Pretending to be fine when inside she's having a meltdown would be child's play to her."

We raced down the sidewalk and

paused where Lily had last been. No sign of her. Roth reached out with his senses, searching for his mate and any traces of where she might have gone.

"She's nowhere to be seen." Lucifer observed. "Perhaps one of us should take to the sky to get a better look of the area."

Roth shook his head. "Lily wouldn't risk being caught flying in New York." He pursed his lips and tried to think of where she might go and how she would get there.

A buzzing startled Roth until he realized it was on his person. Reaching into his pocket, he pulled out his cell phone. He'd almost forgotten he'd brought it with him in case they were separated.

The screen read Ash.

Frowning, Roth put the phone to his ear. "What is it?"

"Hey Roth," Ash started his voice overly cheery. "Can I talk to Lily?"

"Why didn't you call her phone then? And where are you? Your voice is echoing."

"Oh, uh...hehe, about that. We're with Michael scoping out Utopia for Gabriel's next attack." There was some shuffling and words exchanged on his side that Roth couldn't pick up before Ash added, "I was just trying to get a hold of Lily and ask her something. She's not answering her phone so I thought maybe she left it at home. Is she there?"

Roth's eyes narrowed. "What's going on Ash? Lily's not here."

"What do you mean she's not there?" Raven suddenly cried into the phone. "Where is she?"

Jaw tightening, Roth met Lucifer's questioning gaze. "I do not know. She was here and then her father let her out of his sight."

Lucifer threw his hands up and turned his back on him.

"You're her mate, where were you?" Raven accused.

"Now, let us stick to the problem at hand. Why were you wondering about Lily?" Roth redirected the conversation or they would be playing the blame game all day while Hell only knew where Lily had gone.

There was a shuffle and some muttered arguing before Raven sighed and said, "The Wicked Crown is gone. Did Lily take it with her?"

Roth's eyes widened. Had Lily taken the Wicked Crown? If so, how had he not sensed it?

"I'm not sure. I didn't see it." Roth turned to Lucifer. "Could the Wicked Crown shield itself from us?"

Lucifer shrugged. "It is quite possible Lily shielded it herself without realizing it. If she wanted the Wicked Crown bad enough and didn't want us to know about it. Then yes, of course she could."

Roth cursed once more and dragged a hand over his face. "Alright. Let's keep calm. Do not panic yet. We don't know where Lily went or what she is planning on doing."

"Yes, we do." Lucifer stated, causing Roth to frown. "She's going to invade Utopia and take over."

"How do you know that?" Roth asked, not believing him for one second. "Lily wouldn't do that. She has no aspirations to rule over one world let alone two."

Lucifer leveled a look at him. "Because that's what I would do."

"What did he say?" Raven asked, desperation in her voice. "No, give me the phone. I'm trying to listen here, Ash. No, I won't get my own phone. We're mates now, right? What's mine is yours and vice versa, right? So let me use it." There was a long sigh in the background as if Ash had given up the phone. "Come on, Roth. We're in Utopia right now, if Lily is going to do something we need to know."

Roth rubbed his fingertips on his

forehead. He could feel a headache coming on. "Lucifer seems to think that Lily is going to attack Utopia."

"What? Why?"

Letting out a long drawn-out breath, Roth threw a hand up in the air. "Because that's what he would do with the Wicked Crown. So I guess we're coming there."

"You're coming here?" Raven parroted back to him. "Wait...hold on... what was that, Michael? Oh. Okay, good idea."

"What?" Roth asked exasperation, clinging to his voice.

"Michael thinks you should go back to Underworld to see if she rallied the troops first before heading here. Maybe you can cut her off before she makes it to a portal."

Roth hummed. "Yes, you're probably right. We'll head that way now."

"Okay, we'll keep an eye out too. And hey, great reception from here to Earth, right?"

Not answering Raven, Roth hung up the phone and turned to Lucifer only to stop in his tracks at the woman on the sidewalk behind him. Standing behind the king of Hell was his queen and she looked pissed.

"What happened to my daughter, Astaroth?"

Lily

The feel of the Wicked Crown on her head felt right. Lily didn't know how she had gone so long without it on her head. She couldn't even remember the reason why she had taken it off in the first place. She wouldn't let it happen again though.

"Your majesty," a demoness, Lily didn't remember her name, held out a hand toward the table where a selection of outfits for Lily to wear lay.

Humming, Lily approached the table. She had to find the exact right outfit to instill fear and awe in her enemies. She couldn't show up to Utopia looking like a dopey human who didn't know anything.

She paused at a long gown of gauze material. The color was magnificent. An emerald green that shined as the light hit it, making it shimmer in some places. No matter how lovely it was, it wasn't exactly right for an attack on Utopia.

Moving on to the next one, Lily didn't even give it a second thought. The plain slip of a dress wasn't going to instill anything in anyone.

Lily supposed she could just put on the outfit she had worn before. The leather had been quite badass. It would definitely send the right message. However, she wanted to look more like a warrior queen than just a warrior and none of the outfits before her would do that.

Turning her back on the lot of them, she told the demoness, "Take them away. I'll just make something myself."

The demoness hurried to obey.

Lily walked over to the mirror and stared at her reflection. The black crown on her head gleamed in the bedroom light. It needed something that would go with it perfectly. Something that would accent all that it was and send the message that Lily was not someone to be trifled with.

Waving a hand over the front of her, the t-shirt and leggings warped into one piece, lengthening into a dress that hit the floor. The black material was the same as her leggings and wasn't quite right. Humming as she worked, Lily used her magic to shift the material again. This time the black deepened until it was as dark as the endless abyss. A flick of her fingers and a sheen came to it that made it shimmer in the light.

Next Lily focused on the fit of the dress. The skirt was too big and confining for her to move around in easily, especially not good for fighting. She slashed her hand on either side of the skirt, cutting two long slits into either side, allowing her legs to have room to move. The slits stopped at her hips where the material bunched up.

Lily smoothed her hands over the material until it was a dark metal plate that curved over her abdomen and breasts like a chest plate. While she didn't expect to let anyone close enough to harm her, it was better safe than dead. The plate wrapped around the back of her leaving her upper back bare for her wings to come through.

For final touches, she added two metal arm braces to match the breast plate and a pair of boots that came up to her thigh, metal shin plates covering the front of each boot. With that she was ready for battle.

Turning from the mirror, she

stalked away and over to the bed where her purse laid. The demonesses in her room hurried out of her way, a glint of fear in their eyes. Good. If her own people feared her, then it would be easy to inflict the same on those peons in Utopia.

Lily picked up her cell phone and glanced at the screen. Ash had tried to call her. So had Roth...about fifty times. Oh well, it didn't matter. She was queen. They didn't get a say in what she said or did.

Curling her fingers around her phone until the plastic and metal bent and broke beneath the pressure, she let it fall into pieces on the bed. No one would stop her from getting what was rightfully hers, not even her so-called parents.

"Come along," Lily told the demonesses, "We have an army to rally and a new kingdom to claim."

She didn't stop long enough to see if they were following her, Lily walked down the hallway her feet barely touching the floor, her mind solely on the goal ahead. Taking over Utopia. If the angels thought Hell was so bad then she would show them what real Hell was. Then they would see who the real monsters were.

Lily shoved the doors open to the

barracks. She hadn't been in this part of the castle since the first battle getting ready with Bacchi. Her heart faltered slightly at the thought of the demoness. It was only normal that not everyone would survive the attack. It was war after all. Lily shoved it away and put on a confident smile.

"Hello, my soldiers, who is ready to take down Utopia?" The group of soldiers who were doing various things around the barracks, eating, fighting, shining their armor, all looked at her with raised brows. None of them had the vicious gleam in their eyes that she needed. The need for victory. That wouldn't do at all.

"I'm going to need a bit more enthusiasm from you all unless you want to be banished to the human world?" There were a few grumbles. So threats wouldn't do it. "Really? You're going to let those angels come into your home? To your territory and do as they like? Then just leave when they feel like it? What kind of demons are you?" Lily felt a burst of power from the Wicked Crown that filled the room. She wasn't sure what it was doing but it was getting the soldiers' attention on her.

"We cannot stand idly by for Utopia to decide when they want to attack us again. This is our home. Ours. Not theirs. Too long have they looked down on the Underworld. Too long have we played second class to them. It's our turn. Our time. Now, who is ready to take down Utopia?"

There was a pause and then a round of cheers. The demons dropped whatever they were doing and hurried to get ready to take on Utopia. Lily patted herself on the back. Who knew rallying the troops would be so easy? Now they just had to get into Utopia. Hopefully this time they would be the one with the element of surprise and they could take down Gabriel for good.

Lucifer

"I cannot believe you," Lilith said for the hundredth time since she joined our group. "I spend all this time...years...centuries...keeping our daughter safe and the moment you get out of prison you lose her."

"I didn't lose her," Lucifer argued back to his wife as they stalked down the corridor. "She is sneakier than she looks." They had hurried back to the Underworld as soon as they could. Astaroth had taken off ahead to try and keep Lily from leaving first.

Lilith snorted, tossing her violet hair over her shoulder. "You should know a deceiver when you see one. Aren't you supposed to be the king of lies?"

He rolled his eyes toward the sky. "You know very well that some humans made that up. I do not have a deceptive bone in my body." He adjusted the sleeves of his shirt with a sniff. Really. Humans needed to come up with better tales to tell about him, be a bit more creative.

Lilith scoffed while following close behind him. "I happen to remember a specific time where you were masquerading around shaped like a goat man, horns and everything, scaring humans into thinking you were going to damn them."

Lucifer threw his head back and laughed, swinging around to face her. "I had forgotten about that." He smiled at her, for a moment he was nervous about being alone with her for the first time in...geez how long had it been? Lilith, of course, sensed that and took the first step out of his hands by grabbing a hold of his face and kissing him. Then it was like nothing had changed. They hadn't been on the run with their daughter a few decades ago. They were just them.

Wrapping his arms around Lilith, he drew her close to him and savored in the feeling of her body pressed against his. Finally! He couldn't remember how many times he had dreamed of this moment. How many nights he had fallen asleep with the curve of her face in his mind. He ached for Lilith, not just for her body but the soul that lived within her. That fiery spirit that always kept him on his toes.

There was no one in this world who made him feel more alive. That made him feel as if he were the most important person in the world to them than the woman before him. There was a reason he fought against Utopia for her. She was his everything and he wouldn't lose her again.

Withdrawing from the kiss, Lucifer peered into the deep blue of Lilith's eyes. "You have no idea how much I have missed you, my love."

Lilith peered up at him with so much love in her eyes that it made Lucifer ache. "I have missed you too. Now let's go find our daughter."

They hurried down the hallways, searching for Lily and passing all the demons working. Some of them recognized the couple and gasped and bowed, muttering things like 'They have returned!' and others had no clue who they were. It shouldn't come as a surprise, they had been gone for quite a while. Though, it still stung a bit.

Lucifer had spent his life cultivating this world for all the demons so his family would have somewhere to live without persecutions from the angels. Yet here they were with no fucking clue who he was and what he had done for them. It wasn't fair.

They walked around a corner and almost ran into Astaroth.

"Where is she?" Lilith asked before Lucifer could get a word out, her hands tightening on his arm as she clung to him.

"She's not here." Astaroth announced, his wings fluttered with agitation. "From what her maids said, she was here. Rejected all the outfits they made for her and then made something that looked like she was going to battle."

"Okay, where did she go then?" Lilith asked, glancing between Lucifer and Astaroth. "She didn't go to Utopia on her own did she?"

"There is a silver lining there," Astaroth continued, pointing his finger at her. "Apparently, Lily had rallied the troops and they left about half an hour ago to take over Utopia."

"Shit," Lilith gasped and then straightened up with a fierce look. "Then what are we waiting for? Let's go help our baby girl!"

She stormed away before they could stop her. Lucifer exchanged a look with Astaroth and grinned. "Damn it all, I love that woman."

Ash

❧❀❦

"Do you think they will get to her in time?" Raven asked, gripping his arm tight. Ash led her along the corridor behind her father, Michael. The secret passageway seemed to go on forever and ever. It would have been much faster to go straight through like he had before. Though, as Michael had sharply pointed out, that hadn't gotten Ash very far before the league of angels were on him.

"I'm sure Roth will take care of it." Ash patted her hand and sighed. While he did his best to reassure his mate, Ash had doubts himself. He had a bad feeling. It had started the moment he found out the Wicked Crown was missing. Nothing good could come from that crown. He wished Lily had left it right where it was or better yet, at the bottom of the pit.

Michael stopped them before another doorway, this one far more ordinary than the strange mechanism that had brought them to this corridor. Instead of working out some kind of puzzle on the doorway, Michael stuck his hand inside the front of his shirt and withdrew a necklace. On the necklace was a silver key. Slipping the key into the lock, he gave it a turn until it clicked and he pushed the door open.

"And we are here," Michael waved a hand through the doorway as if to ask them to go first. When Ash and Raven stared at him, not moving forward, Michael dropped his arm. "Are you afraid? I promise you there's no one on the other side of this doorway. It leads to my cellar. The only thing you're likely to come across is a scatous."

Ash arched his brow. "What's that?"

"It's like a mouse," Raven explained, taking a step forward. "If a mouse had a long-split tongue and scales."

Ash shuddered. "I think I'd rather face an angel horde."

Raven rolled her eyes and waved an arm over her shoulder at him. "Alright, my fearless mate. Let's go."

Ash held his breath as Raven

walked through the doorway. There was silence and then a blood curdling scream. "Raven!" Ash rushed forward, his jaw elongating and smoke coming from between his sharpened teeth.

Pawing at the ground, Ash snarled and searched the room for his mate and whoever dared to touch her. All he found was Raven laughing herself silly. Gaped at her, Ash resumed his human form and growled. "That's not funny."

Michael walked in behind him. "I found it amusing."

Raven snickered and approached Ash, "I'm sorry, Ash. I couldn't help myself. You were acting so skittish, I just wanted to lighten the mood." She wrapped her arms around Ash's shoulders and pressed her lips to his cheek. "Thank you for coming to my rescue though. I have no fear knowing you will be there to protect me."

Ash let himself smile slightly before kissing her back. "I don't know about protecting you, you do a fairly good job of that yourself. If anything, I'll at least be there to have your back or at the very least avenge you."

Chuckling, Raven squeezed him tightly before releasing him to follow after her father. "Come on before Michael finds something else to poke fun at you for."

"And who's fault is that?" Ash muttered after her.

They trotted up a pair of stairs where Michael had disappeared. Ash tucked his hands into his pockets and had a look around. This would probably be the last time he'd have a chance to see inside Michael's house. The last time Ash had been completely focused on getting Raven back and he hadn't taken the time to look properly. He was curious to see what an archangel's home looked like.

Coming upon a hallway with several doors, Ash couldn't help but give the nearest door a little wiggle. Locked. Damn it. He wandered on and did the same to the next door.

"What are you doing?" Raven asked, arching a brow at him with her arms crossed over her chest.

Ash shrugged. "Nothing. Just taking a look around."

"What exactly are you looking for?" Raven smirked, tucking her hair behind her ear.

Lifting his shoulders and dropping them once more, Ash muttered, "I don't know. Maybe a trove of jewels. Fountains of milk and honey?"

Raven covered her mouth as she laughed. "Not only is that stuff the humans make up not true, but why in the world would my father keep those things inside of his house?"

Ash rubbed the back of his neck. "Hey, how should I know? I don't know what these pretentious jerkwads do in their houses."

Eyes narrowed, Raven scowled. "I happen to be one of those pretentious jerkwads."

"Not the same and you know it. You're hardly the same." Ash gestured at her with a grin and then wagged his brows. "After all, I wouldn't be caught dead doing that thing you like with my tongue to -"

"Okay, okay," Raven rushed over to him and clamped her hands over his mouth. "We don't need to go into detail here in my father's house where he can overhear. He still doesn't exactly like you, you know."

"He doesn't?" Ash asked, his voice muffled behind her hand. Raven dropped her hand. "Why not?"

Raven shrugged, both hands open before her. "How should I know? I hardly know the man. But if it counts for anything, I like you." She winked at him and bumped him with her hip.

"Only like me?" Ash cocked a brow and chased after her. "I'd think after all we've done together, I'd at least have earned a bit more than like."

Raven wrinkled her nose at him. "Well, it depends on the time of day. At the moment, I like you. When you're not trying to embarrass me in my father's house, then perhaps I care for you a bit more than like."

Ash shook his head, unable to hold back the grin on his face. Oh, this woman. How he loved her.

Michael

❧❦☙

He could hear everything they were saying. If he was honest with himself, it was disturbing to hear his daughter's mate talk about debasing her the way he was. However, he could only assume it was normal.

Why, Michael remembered when he and Raven's mother were together. Were they not all over each other as much as they could be? Did he not lavish her with unending attention and make love to her as often as he could? If she had not been human, Michael could have seen himself spending the rest of eternity with her. Unfortunately, those things were not in the cards for him and Raven's mother was taken shortly after Raven's birth by some human illness or another.

Michael let out a long breath and

turned toward the living area. He wanted to give them a moment to themselves. With Lily on her way to declare war on Utopia, who knew when they would get the chance again. In fact, Michael should gather his own forces and get ready for the fight. If Lily was going to go up against Gabriel, what kind of angel would he be to let her go up against him alone?

"Your grace," a low-level angel who served in Michael's home came into the living area. The surprise on her face showed that she obviously didn't expect him back.

"Martha." Michael inclined his head. "I'm going to need you to get the word out to my troops. We move in the next hour. They need to get ready and be here by then."

Martha's brows furrowed. "Is there something the matter, your grace?"

"Nothing to worry yourself about." He waved her off, shifting toward the trunk by the door that held some of his weapons. "Pass my message along and then I want you to get out of here. Head to the outskirts and keep away until you get word."

"From you?" Martha questioned, her voice still showing uncertainty.

Michael nodded. "Me or someone else, my daughter, perhaps."

"Your daughter?" Martha gasped.

Turning slightly toward her, Michael swung his sword across the air. "Yes, my daughter, Martha. I know it's been a while since you saw her. I didn't exactly let anyone take care of her but me last time. The timing was too sensitive to allow anyone to know she was here."

"No, your grace. Your daughter. She's here."

"Oh," Michael turned around, feeling a bit foolish. "Yes, she is. This is my daughter, Raven, and her...her mate." He smacked his lips, the word feeling strange on his tongue.

Ash snorted. "And here I thought you were kidding about his dislike for me."

Raven nudged the hellhound with her elbow and smirked. "He'll warm up to you. I did after all."

"Yeah, but I don't think how I warmed you up will work on your father."

Michael grimaced. "Please, no more bedroom talk about my daughter. I think I have had more than a lifetime's worth of it. I don't want my last thoughts before going into the afterlife to be of what you have done with that hellhound."

"Funny," Ash grinned wolfishly at

Raven, "sounds like the best way to go out to me."

Raven lifted her eyes to the ceiling and muttered something under her breath before turning her gaze back to Michael. "So what's the plan? Just sit here and wait for Lily to show up and start a war?"

Michael twisted back toward the trunk. "That would hardly be productive. Martha is going to send word to my troops. That way we at least have a fighting chance if she does start anything."

"Which she will," Ash interjected.

"How do you know that?" Raven inquired.

"Because I've heard the stories of when Lucifer ruled and what the Wicked Crown did to him." Michael glanced up to see Ash give a visible shudder. "That thing is not good for anyone."

"You have to admit, it did give Lily the upper hand with Gabriel," Michael mentioned, pulling a few more swords from the trunk. He sat them on the side table next to him and kept searching through the trunk. He knew it was in here somewhere.

"Yeah, but at what cost?" Ash countered.

A shadow appeared over Michael's shoulder. "What are you doing?"

Michael didn't look up at his daughter while he rummaged around in the trunk. "I'm trying to find...ah...there it is!" He grabbed the item he was looking for and lifted it up, pivoting around so fast that Raven stumbled back from him.

"Oh, cool, a sword." Ash pointed at the pile on the side table. "Don't you have enough of them already?"

"This is not just any sword." Michael held this sword with reverence and stepped forward. "This is the sword..." he swung the blade and blue, white flames appeared down the line of the edge. "This sword is one of the few swords left imbued with our leader's glory."

Raven gaped at him. "And you had it stored in your trunk where anyone could find it?"

Michael cocked his head to the side and swung the sword again putting the flame out. "If I put it on display or hide it behind wards then it would draw someone's attention to it. However, if I put it along with several other swords out in the open where anyone could take it, then it becomes unimportant and someone is less likely to try and take it."

"Ah, got it." Ash bobbed his head and then looked at Raven with wide eyes.

Sighing, Michael sheathed the sword and sat down at a nearby table. "Do not worry yourself about it. It will only cause you a headache and we need you in top shape for what's to come."

Raven sat at the seat next to him and placed her hands on the table in front of her. "So, what now? Do you have more secret passageways? Should we train some?"

Michael shook his head. "No, no more secret passages. No training. We don't want to wear ourselves out before the battle."

Ash stepped up behind Raven, placing a hand on her shoulder. "Then what do we do?"

Crossing his arms over his chest and closing his eyes as he leaned back in his chair, Michael stated, "Now...we wait."

Lily

Nothing sounded better than the sound of her army marching on Utopia. Not the sound of the rain falling on the concrete, not even the little sounds Roth made in the back of his throat when she licked him in just the right places, could compare to the sheer pleasure the sounds of her army moving gave Lily.

She flew overhead watching the demons march across the fields she had entered for the first time feeling like days ago rather than only years. Trampling those gorgeous flowers beneath their feet as they made their way to the portal Lily was going to open.

After she had gotten her army together, Lily had the problem of finding a portal to Utopia. She couldn't very well bring them through Earth first to the portal Ash had found. There had to be another way for them to get there. After all, Gabriel had done it, why couldn't she?

"Stop here," she called out to the army below. Without hesitation, they stopped. Lily smiled. Perfect. Flying down to the head of the army, she focused on the area before her. She had never made a portal before but now was as good of time as any to figure it out. After all, the Wicked Crown told her it was easy and with it backing her, there was no way she could fail.

Lifting a hand up, Lily pictured in her mind what she wanted to do. The image of the shimmering swirling portal she had come through with Roth so long ago came to her mind. Pushing her magic outward, she willed it into being. Lily thought of a way to get into Utopia with all her might, willing her magic to make it so.

After a few moments, a small swirl of air appeared in the center of where her hand was pointing. Encouraged by its appearance Lily pushed even further, asking the Wicked Crown to give her the strength to make it real, make it bigger. After all, she had a whole army to fit through, not even a fly could make it through that tiny hole as it was now.

Inch by inch it grew beneath her ministrations until finally it grew into a full-size portal. More than that. It was as long as a football field and just as high. The army could easily come through all at once rather than being bottlenecked at the entrance.

Lily's skin buzzed with excitement. This was it. She was going to get revenge on Gabriel and take over all of Utopia. Then who knew where else she might go. She could become the queen of everything.

The thought of being the Queen of Everything spurred her on. She poured her magic into both hands recreating the energy swords from her first fight with Gabriel. Lily turned to the troops and lifted them both in the air. "For the Underworld!" Before pivoting on her heel and pushing off the ground, her wings flapped hard behind her as she shoved through the portal, the army cheering at her back. The pounding of the army followed her into the portal and onto the other side.

The light shone brightly down on them as Lily led them into a large field in Utopia. If this had been any other time, Lily might have stopped to take in the very place the humans called

Heaven. However, the luscious grass and pure blue sky did nothing to sway the need for vengeance in Lily's heart.

Not sure where she was going or if she was even leading her army in the right direction, Lily let the Wicked Crown decide for her.

There, it said, in the distance.

Lily squinted at what the Wicked Crown wanted her to see. Beyond a wall of trees that surrounded the field laid a wall. The pristine white stones of the wall were so bright that it almost hurt to look at them. Lily used her hand to cover her eyes slightly trying to get a better look.

"Your majesty?" A nearby demon asked. "Do we proceed?"

Lily caught sight of a few angels walking along the wall, almost the size of ants from how far they were from her. Even if Gabriel was not there, it was as good of place as any to start her siege.

"Forward!" She called out, letting her wings lift her into the air. The demons moved behind her in tandem. There weren't quite as many demons as she'd hoped for her army but she would have to make do and take out the majority with her own powers.

A shout and then a gathering of voices could be heard the moment they came close enough into view of the angels. A trumpet sounded somewhere in the keep. Dozens of angels poured over the wall, their wings flapping madly in the air as they came at them.

A jolt of adrenaline rushed through Lily's body and she let out a mighty cry before pushing her way forward. Without stopping she slashed through angels one after another, each of them falling to the ground and the demons waiting below.

Gnashing her teeth at the oncoming angels, she preened as they faltered at the sight of her taking down their brethren.

"Come on, you cowards!" Lily swung her blades in the air before her. "You can come into my kingdom and attack me but you run when I come after you? I don't think so!"

Using her swords she shoved energy into them, swinging them so that the balls of power launched themselves from the tip of each sword. They smashed into the wall, shattering the stones and bringing down angels with it. People screamed and all Lily could think was more, more, more!

Ash

"Shit." He jumped to his feet at the loud bang that reverberated the whole house. "What was that?"

Michael calmly stood to his feet. "I would say that is your friend."

"Lily?" Ash gaped, looking at Raven. "She's here already?"

Raven pursed her lips. "You so often underestimate her. Did you really think she'd be stupid enough to let herself be caught?"

Ash scowled. "Well, no, but I thought we'd have a little more warning. At least, have back up here." Sighing, he picked up one of the swords Michael had laid out. "What do we do?"

Michael shifted out of his chair and adjusted the sword at his waist. "The only thing we can do. Try to stop them."

"But who are we stopping?" Raven asked smartly. "Lily? Or Gabriel?"

Ash raised his hand, "I vote for Gabriel."

Michael frowned. "Both of them. Lily we know is here. Gabriel may not even be in the area."

"Yes, he is."

They all turned to Martha standing in the doorway of the living area.

"I thought I told you to go somewhere safe," Michael chastised the woman.

Martha didn't so much as flinch at the stern look on Michael's face. Apparently, she was used to it. Ash would have to ask her how she did that.

"I know you did and I didn't." Martha moved further into the room, her hands twisting her apron in her fists. "When I went to deliver your message, I saw Gabriel there. He was already trying to gather more forces to attack the heir again."

A growl came from Michael that would rival even Ash's. "Barely back a moment and the bastard is already trying to poach my people? Where were they headed?"

Martha's gaze heated. "Toward the

glade where an army of demons are waiting."

Shoving away from the table, Michael hurried around the room grabbing a spear and shield before tossing them toward Raven. She caught them beautifully, of course. Michael muttered to himself before barking out, "How many traitors?"

"At least half, your grace."

"That's a lot," Ash couldn't help but point out. "Are you sure this isn't partly your fault? I mean, haven't you been treating them, right?"

"Ash," Raven hissed.

He shrugged. "What? It's a legitimate question. If your father had kept his people happy maybe, we wouldn't have to fight them now."

Michael spun around, stalking toward Ash until he was inches before his face. "It has nothing to do with how well I treat my people and everything to do with fear. Something Gabriel is well tuned in. He could make a child fear its own mother with just the right words. Anything can be spun to your benefit if you know where to hit the hardest."

"So you're saying they are fighting because Gabriel tricked them?" Raven clarified, still glowering at Ash.

"He didn't need to." Michael shook

his head and started for the door. "All he needed to tell them was their home was in danger and they would have gathered arms to defend it. And your dear friend, Lily, is an invader and from the Underworld at that."

"But Gabriel attacked first!" Ash tried to argue to no avail.

"Doesn't matter to them. They weren't there." Michael grabbed the door handle and pulled it open. Another boom shook the house as he said, "With his army and part of my own fighting for him, it's going to be an all-out slaughter."

Then Michael darted out into the street. Raven and Ash exchanged a look before she started for the door.

"Wait!" He caught up to her and grabbed her hand.

"You heard him." Raven waved her shield at the doorway. "We have to get out there or there will be no one left to even live in the Underworld."

"I know," Ash breathed and squeezed his eyes shut for a second before peering into Raven's eyes. "I just want a moment. A moment for us before we go out there and risk our lives again. A moment to remember how much I love you and how happy I am that I finally found you. My mate."

Raven's gaze softened and she

leaned into him, placing her face against his neck. Ash wrapped his arms around her, holding her tightly to him. He never wanted to let her go.

Sadly, after another blast that sent dust particles flying onto them, Ash and Raven released one another. He brushed his thumb across her cheek and smiled down at her. "This isn't the end, Nephilim. We're going to go out there and kick some angel ass and then I'm going to take you home and marry you."

Raven threw her head back and laughed. "Is that a proposal? Because it needs work."

Ash kissed her soundly on the lips. "I'll do it as many times as you want. Let's just live through this first."

Raven smirked. "With you and my father backing me up? There's no way I'm going to die." Raven tweaked his nose and raced toward the door.

"Don't jinx it." Ash growled, chasing after her.

Ash barely made it out the door before he was blasted back against the wall of the house. He covered a hand over his eyes and tried to see through the dust around them at who kept hitting them.

Unable to make anything out, Ash followed Raven's silhouette through the dust cloud. People screamed and ran in the opposite direction. Angels armed themselves and headed toward the wall surrounding the city. He caught up to Raven at the entrance gate where it had all but been destroyed, leaving a pile of rubble in its wake.

"Do you see her?" Raven asked over the chaos.

"No." Ash shook his head. "Any sign of Gabriel? Or better yet Roth?"

"No sign of them either." A blast hit the wall next to them and they ducked out of the way. Coughing at the debris, Raven pointed out. "Well, I think we found Lily."

Ash followed her finger toward a flying figure overhead, a menacing energy coming off of her. Through the clouds of dust, Ash could make out the two glowing swords she wielded, slashing one and then the other through the air as she set energy bombs at the city.

"What is she trying to do? Destroy the place?" Ash scowled and stepped over the rumble.

He held a hand out to Raven helping her over a large piece as she said, "I don't know. Maybe it's easier to take over a kingdom if they're all dead?"

Ash grimaced at the thought. That

would be something the Wicked Crown would suggest. He couldn't imagine the girl he'd met at NYU who had been so upset by the loss of life because of her being able to cause such carnage. Was she not thinking of the innocents she was hurting?

"Come on," Raven charged forward. "If we can get to her first then maybe we can end all this madness."

Ash followed after her, dodging demons left and right. He didn't want to hurt his own people but they also didn't seem to realize he was one of them. Ash had come out of the gates so that didn't look particularly good.

"Back off," he snarled, letting his face transform partly to get the demons to realize he was one of them. Which worked for the most part except some of them still tried to attack Raven so then he was off trying to protect her.

They finally reached the ground beneath Lily and Raven released her wings. Before she could shoot up into the sky, Ash caught sight of something that had him grabbing Raven's arm and pulling her back.

"What is it? This is our chance?" Raven stared at him in confusion.

Ash shook his head pointing a little bit away in the sky. "It's too late. Gabriel is already here."

Gabriel

The impertinence of the child. To think she would come here to his own kingdom and try to attack him?

Never mind that he had done the exact same thing.

It was different though. What he did was for the good of all of Utopia and the rest of the world. The heir had to be destroyed for them to be safe. No one would blame him for what he had done. For all Gabriel had to do to fulfill his duty.

If this little girl thought that she would be able to defeat him here when she couldn't in her own realm, then she was even more insane than he thought before.

Gabriel watched from afar, taking in the battlefield before deciding how he would proceed. Had there been this many demons last time? No. He didn't think so.

Counting up the demons attacking from below, Gabriel thanked all that was holy that he had been able to bring on some of Michael's troops over to his side. It hadn't taken much to convince them to join the cause. A few well-placed words here and a touch of fear there and the next thing he knew Gabriel had rounded out his army with another legion or so.

"Your grace," a nearby angel hovered by him. "How would you like us to proceed?"

Gabriel narrowed his eyes on the battlefield, his gaze zeroing in on the two unfavorables making their way toward the front of the demon horde. If Michael's spawn was down there, then the archangel himself couldn't be far behind. He'd have to keep an eye out for him, his brother tended to like to come in at the last possible moment. When it would cause the most damage.

Curious as to why the hellhound and Nephilim were heading toward the other side rather than trying to fight the angels coming at their people, Gabriel searched out the one causing him the biggest headache.

Lily.

That little bitch was going to destroy the whole city before she even got to face him and she didn't seem to care in the slightest. In any other situation, Gabriel would be awed by the massive amounts of power she was swinging from her energy swords, demolishing everything in its wake. However, as of now, Gabriel could only focus on how he would take the little bitch down.

To the angel, Gabriel commanded, "Take your troops and come along the right flank. Have the ones we acquired from Michael go along the left flank. I will take on the demon scums' leader."

Without argument the angel took to the sky to deliver Gabriel's message. Gabriel turned back to the problem before him. How to destroy the heir without putting himself in danger? Then his gaze fell on the two below her flying form once more. Could they possibly be trying to stop her? A wicked thought came to Gabriel's mind. The perfect way to get the heir off kilter so he could defeat her and all of hell would be at his mercy.

Gabriel's wings pushed down as his feet thrust from the ground, taking to the air at an alarming speed. He had to get to the heir before her little friends did. That was the only way his plan would work. The last thing he needed was for backup to come for her. Gabriel knew that Lucifer was still out there and if his child was here then he couldn't be too far behind. Once they were at her side then it would all be over and Gabriel wouldn't stand a chance.

Roth

The fighting had already commenced by the time they had arrived. Roth could hear the battle from the portal and see the smoke rising up from behind the trees.

"We're too late," Lilith murmured in despair.

"Not yet, my dear." Lucifer consoled her. "We can still stop this before we lose our daughter again."

Roth turned to them both. "We need a plan. One of us should focus on getting Lily to leave. The others should keep Gabriel and whoever else is out there away from her so she doesn't get tempted into fighting more."

Lilith frowned and glanced at her husband. "In this circumstance, I would normally say a parent should talk her down but seeing as neither one of us have been in her life long enough for her to care what we think, it obviously should be you, Astaroth."

"I agree." Lucifer nodded. "She won't listen to us. It was us that made her take off in the first place. The only person she might listen to is you."

"Very well," Roth inclined his head and focused back on the battlefield in the distance. "What will the two of you do?"

Lucifer cracked his knuckles. "I would like to take a swing at my brother again. Give him a taste of his own medicine. I do owe him for locking me up for the last few centuries."

Lilith let out a sigh. "Please don't get yourself killed after I just got you back."

"She's right," Roth said over his shoulder. "Aim for distraction, not for killing. I'm not saying you can't kill him. Just don't make it your main goal. We don't want any sacrifices for the greater good here today."

Lucifer pursed his lips but jerked his head once in understanding.

"Good. Now that we have a plan. Let's go get our girl." Roth took to the sky with Lucifer carrying Lilith close behind. His heart hammered in his chest the closer they came to the battlefield. Roth had spent all this time, all these centuries looking, searching for Lily, he wasn't about to lose her now. Not when he was so close to having their happy ending.

"Look, there." Lucifer called behind him and Roth's gaze searched out what Lucifer was pointing out. "There's Lily. And of course, Gabriel has already found her."

A low growl rumbled through Roth's chest at the mention of that wretched archangel anywhere near his mate. He pushed his muscles harder, making his wings beat faster. He had to get to Lily before Gabriel could hurt her or worse, Lily did something unforgivable.

Roth broke through the trees and found himself at the back of the demon army. The front line mingled with the angels attacking from the other end. It was easy for Roth to find Lily high above the fighting, her energy swords locked with Gabriel's weapon. If possible, Roth fought to make himself go faster. He didn't know what he would do once he got to Lily, he just knew that he had to be there by her side. Everyone was relying on him to get her to listen to him. To get her to find herself somewhere inside away from the influence of the Wicked Crown. He could see it gleaming on her head even from where he flew.

Once he was close enough, Roth could make out the words being exchanged between the two of them.

"You really think you can defeat me here?" Gabriel laughed, throwing his weight into the sword and clashed up against Lily's. "You couldn't defeat me in your world, you don't have a chance of defeating me here."

Roth wanted to call out to her. The words were in his throat but he swallowed them down. Anything he said now would just distract her from the fight and that could be deadly.

Instead, Roth forced himself to stop a few paces back from where they fought. He winced with every clash of their powers. A shout from below caused Roth's gaze to shoot down to the ground. Raven and Ash stood on the ground, fighting off the angels as they came hurtling toward them. Roth didn't see Michael anywhere in sight. That didn't mean the archangel wasn't nearby.

Eyes darting to Lily for a brief moment, Roth made the decision. He aimed for the ground and came up behind Ash just as an angel tried to gut him from behind. "Need a hand?"

"Finally, you show up," Ash called

over his shoulder before thrusting his weapon into the next angel coming at him. "It took you long enough."

"Would you two stop jabbering?" Raven called out, throwing her spear once before swinging her wings around to knock back the next onslaught of angels. "We need to get to Lily."

"How exactly do you expect to do that?" Roth asked, shooting an energy ball at a pack of angels, hitting them back. "If any of us distract her from fighting Gabriel, we could be writing her death."

"We can't just do nothing," Raven snapped back and met Roth in the middle of a pause. "One of us has to distract Gabriel so that the other can grab Lily."

Ash turned to them. "Roth will grab Lily. She'll listen to him."

"Then I'll distract Gabriel," Raven stated, her gaze going to the archangel above them. Before they could tell her otherwise, Raven shot up to the sky, her spear in her hand.

"Shit. There she goes again." Ash scowled after her. "When will that woman ever learn to stop leaving me behind."

Roth chuckled. "I know how you feel."

"Well, then..." Ash glanced around

the battlefield a grin grew across his face until his mouth split and his flaming snout came into place. "Time for a change of pace." His whole body shook as smoke and flames overcame him. The angels stood back for a moment, fear and awe on their face before they jumped back as Ash's full hellhound form came barreling out of the smoke around him.

Roth smiled at the hellhound who seemed to have things well in hand now before taking to the sky. If Raven was going to be the bait, then Roth could at least do his part to draw Lily away from the battle. And perhaps finish this battle before too many more lives were lost.

Lily

She had Gabriel on the run. He couldn't hold up much longer against her, she could tell. His power was faltering and sweat rolled down his face. This was her moment. Her moment to get revenge for all the pain and heartache the archangel had caused her and her family. Her moment to take not only Utopia but soon the rest of the universe.

"Hey, dickwad!" Raven shouted behind Gabriel pulling both of their attention to her. "I've got a score to settle with you."

"No, you don't," Lily scowled. "This is my fight! Go find your own."

Raven ignored her and came charging at Gabriel. The archangel shifted his focus from fighting Lily to dodging the spear pointed at his chest.

Lily growled and powered up her swords ready to knock her friend down a few pegs for getting in her way. Before she could follow through with her plans, a pair of strong arms looped through her arms and jerked her against a familiar warm chest.

"Let me go, Roth," Lily snarled at her mate, struggling against his hold. "I have to do this. I have to kill Gabriel."

Roth held her tighter, causing her wings to struggle to flap and keep herself up in the air. "No, you don't. You don't have to do any of this Lily. You can just come home. With me."

Lily shoved away from Roth with a kick to his shin. Roth made an oof sound before releasing her. "Don't get in my way," she warned and spun away from him only to find Roth in her way once more.

"Or what?" Roth taunted her. "You'll kill me?"

The Wicked Crown whispered to her, telling her she didn't need him. That all she needed was to kill Gabriel. To take over Utopia. To be queen of everything!

"Come on, Lily Morgan Star." Roth held his arms open to either side. "This is your chance. Take me out, kill me, and then you can go on savaging this world to your heart's content."

Lily lifted her sword, her jaw clenched.

"But will the crown really be satisfied then?" Roth continued on, not paying any mind that she was just this close to the side of following through with her threat. "Will it be over once you get what you want? Revenge on Gabriel and Utopia? Will you finally be happy then?"

Frowning at Roth, Lily considered his words. "You can't think that I should just let him go, do you? He has to pay for what he's done."

Roth shook his head. "But not like this, my love. Not by destroying innocents just like they did to you. Not by ripping families apart because you have a grudge against their leader."

Lily paused and processed what he was saying. Her eyes finally opened up wide enough to see the damage she had done to the city beyond. The screams of people fleeing her attacks filled her ears and she felt sick. She'd done this. She'd been the cause of even more people to lose their lives. All she wanted was to avenge her family. To give Gabriel exactly what he deserved. But she was so blinded by her hatred of him and needed to take over that she let the Wicked Crown sneak into her mind again and warp what she wanted into more. It wanted power, no matter the cost.

"It's not too late, Lily." Roth held out his hand to her. "Come with me and we can leave this place. Come with me and we can go home and be free and happy, together."

Lily wanted to. She wanted to take his hand and go with him. She wanted so many things that he had said to her. It was the damn crown though. It pushed at her will. Telling her that she could have all those things but first, she had to take over Utopia. She would never be safe. Never be free as long as Gabriel still lived.

Ready to give up, Lily lifted her gaze to Roth only to see Gabriel and Raven fighting behind him. For a second, she saw double. Roth pleading with her to leave and Gabriel taunting her to come get him. Her mind kept shifting back to Roth and she had almost let her energy swords go...she almost let it all go and left with him.

"Raven!" Lily called out just as Gabriel caught Raven under the chin and slammed her own spear into her chest. Jaw clenched, Lily gripped her swords tightly and shoved toward the archangel, Roth all but forgotten in her pursuit.

"Lily!" Roth's voice called after her

but she ignored him. While Gabriel's back was turned, Lily swung her swords at him. Her swords slashed through bone and muscle, catching hold of each wing in an x-shaped motion that left Gabriel screaming out, his hands dropping the spear and Raven skewered on the end along with it.

With his wings no longer keeping him up in the air, Gabriel fell from the sky grappling at air. Lily watched him with deep satisfaction as Gabriel plummeted to the ground. He landed with a thump so loud that it shook the battlefield. Before Lily could finish the job, Michael came out of nowhere and plunged his flaming sword into Gabriel's heart, effectively killing the archangel in one blow.

It wasn't enough. Lily could feel the power pulsating through her. Killing Gabriel wasn't enough. She needed more. She needed to rule over them all.

"Lily," Roth murmured near her, slowly coming up beside her without her noticing. "That's enough. He's gone. He's dead. You can go home now."

Lily shook with the need to let the Wicked Crown do as it willed. Her eyes watered with the effort to keep from doing what the crown wanted. What finally broke the Wicked Crown's hold on her was the sight of Raven, broken on the ground, Ash fighting his way through the army of angels to get to her.

Gasping, Lily's hand came up to her mouth, her swords disappearing without a thought. "What have I done?"

"It wasn't your fault," Roth told her, placing a hand on her shoulder and urging her down to the ground. "This was Gabriel's doing. Not yours."

"But if I hadn't..." Lily gasped, her lungs pulling in air rapidly. "If I hadn't come here. If I had only listened..."

When they landed on the ground, Roth pulled her into his arms, her wings folding down behind her. "Shush now. It'll all be alright."

"Maybe I can save her," Lily asked, lifting her head from Roth's chest. "The crown has so many powers, maybe I can use it to bring her back."

"No," Ash answered, shifting into his human form to stand over Raven with such pain in his eyes. "Do not use the crown on her. Who knows what it could do to her? No, that thing needs to go back where it belongs."

"Oh, God...fuck, Ash, I'm...I'm so sorry." Lily reached toward him but he stepped back from her, his eyes on Raven.

Ash shook his head. "Like Roth said, it wasn't your fault. Gabriel did this and Raven chose to be the one to go after him. Do not put more guilt on yourself than you already have. Put the blame where it goes." They all turned to the body of Gabriel now burning into nothing from Michael's sword.

The angels near them stared at the sight of their leader dead. Michael turned to them and called out, "Go home. Do not speak of what was done here. If I hear about it from anyone, you will have me to deal with."

The angels didn't even hesitate this time before they flew back to the city. The demons hung around a bit longer, seeming unsure what to do now. Lily couldn't bring herself to command them again. She'd done enough damage.

Thankfully, her father chose that moment to appear amongst the fleeing angels. "You have done enough. Go home. There's nothing else for you here."

The demons peered at Lucifer and her mother, who tentatively came out from behind him as if unsure of her place there. Then the demons turned to her. Confliction appeared on their faces. Did they listen to Lucifer or to Lily?

Tired, Lily pulled away from Roth long enough to tell them. "Go. Do as he says. Thank you for your help."

Once there was no one left but their group, Michael stood over his daughter with a frown on his lips. "Now, to right a wrong."

Ash

The pain in Ash's chest was excruciating. It was worse than the time he had found Raven missing. Worse than not knowing if she was alive or dead. The sight of his mate, bleeding and dead on the ground was enough to make him want to tear everything around him apart.

Ash resisted. No good would come from him going on a rampage and destroying more of Utopia than Lily had already done. There was nothing left for him to do but come to terms with his mate's sacrifice.

"No one can kill me with you two having my back," Ash mimicked Raven's words back to her motionless body. "You're such a fucking liar." He rubbed his eyes and pulled in several deep breaths. He wouldn't break down here. Not in front of Lily. She felt shit enough he was sure about it, there was no reason to add to it with his own agony.

"Stand back," Michael instructed everyone, coming down to his knees beside Raven.

"What do you think you can do that the crown can't?" Ash asked, unable to keep the growl from his voice. He'd had about enough angels for one day.

Michael didn't answer him, holding his hands over Raven's body. Roth watched him with growing agitation. Why bother trying to heal her now? He could have shown up sooner and saved her from dying in the first place. Nothing was going to come of this but more heartbreak and Ash didn't think he could handle any more of it. He'd already lost Raven twice, he wouldn't get his hopes up to only lose her again.

"Brother," Lucifer stepped forward, his hand hovering over Michael's shoulder. "Are you sure?"

Michael didn't remove his gaze from his daughter. "There are many things I should have done for my daughter and didn't. This is one thing I can do for her. Let me do it."

"But -"

"Wouldn't you do the same in place for your daughter?" Michael cut him off, his gaze flicking briefly over to Lily before focusing back on Raven. "My life means nothing if I cannot use it to keep my child safe. I have failed already. Now let me fix it."

Ash stared at the archangel, beginning to realize what he was doing. "Michael. No. As much as I want Raven back, she wouldn't want this. She wouldn't want you to give your life for hers."

Michael offered Ash a small smile. "I am glad that my daughter will have you there for her. I did not approve of you at first, though what father would approve of anyone who took their little girl away from them? I have to say that I am content in knowing you will be there for her when I am gone. Please take care of her and help her to understand."

"I don't understand." Lily murmured nearby. "What is he doing?"

Roth clung to Lily tightly. "He's pouring his power, his life force into Raven. Basically, exchanging her life for his own."

"Wait, what?" Lily gaped at Michael, her throat bobbing. Ash knew how she felt. The archangel was making the ultimate sacrifice and while none of them wanted to see him do it, they couldn't bring themselves to stop him either.

"I will make sure that Raven knows what you have done for her." Ash swallowed down his emotions, keeping his eyes locked on the male before him. "Our children will know of it too."

Michael lifted his eyes to the sky and a golden light enveloped him as a look of pure contentment came over his face. As his eyes fluttered closed, Raven's opened once more. Confusion came over her face as she stared up at her father and then panic poured into her expression.

"Dad, no!" Raven grabbed at his hands and scrambled to her knees, throwing her arms around her father. "What the hell are you doing? Are you crazy?"

Michael wrapped his arms around her, holding her to him. "Do not worry for me, daughter. I will see you again. On the other side." Then his form flickered and shimmered before disappearing all together, leaving Raven holding onto air.

Tears poured down Raven's face and Ash hurried over to her, pulling her to his chest. "It's alright, Raven. I'm here. It'll all be okay." Ash stared over Raven's head at the others as she cried into his chest. His heart was so full of love for her and yet he knew how much she ached for the loss of her father. Ash couldn't explain how grateful he was for Michael's sacrifice and yet hate the archangel for making his mate suffer so.

"Why did he disappear like that?" Lily murmured to Roth. "Do all angels disappear when they die?"

Ash would have told her to not ask about that right now but he could tell Raven was listening and if he was honest, he wanted to know as well.

Lucifer was the one who answered. "No. We don't disappear the same way Michael did. In the same aspect as humans when we die, our bodies remain unless destroyed..." he peered over at what remained of Gabriel's body. "However, Michael didn't just give up his life energy for Raven. He poured all his power into her. Essentially making her an archangel now."

Ash stared down at his mate. "Do you feel any different?"

"I just died and came back to life, what do you think?" she retorted with a growl. Then paused and seemed to assess herself. "I do feel different. Lighter almost. Not so...grounded?"

"That would be your father's powers," Lucifer explained, wrapping his arm around Lilith. It seemed all of them were worried their loved one would suddenly disappear on them again. "Your human side is still there but the things that would hold you down before won't be as prominent now. You'll have to be careful with learning to use your new abilities."

Raven nodded against Ash's chest, then turned her head up. "Can we go home now?"

Ash peered down at her and brushed her tears away with his thumbs. "Yes, we can. I mean -" he looked over at Lily. "If that's okay with you, your majesty?"

Lily stiffened against Roth. "Please don't call me that."

"Why not? It's true," Ash continued, "The troops wouldn't leave because of Lucifer's command. They listen to you now and so does the rest of the Underworld. I think that effectively makes you queen."

Letting out a long sigh, Lily didn't argue any further and bobbed her head. "Yeah, let's go home."

Lily

Lily laid her head on Roth's chest, her fingers swirling through his chest hair. They had only been home for a few hours and still Lily's mind kept lingering on the battlefield. Her head felt light and as if something were missing without the Wicked Crown on it. Thankfully, it was back where it belonged in the all black room, imprisoned behind more wards than even Lily could break.

It wasn't enough. Lily could still feel the influence of the Wicked Crown scratching at the back of her mind. She wanted to pretend like she had control of it. That she could keep the whispers of the crown at bay but with Raven's death and rebirth so close to the surface of her mind, Lily couldn't pretend to be strong anymore.

"I can't ever leave again, can I?"

Roth placed his hand on her shoulder and rubbed it soothingly. "It probably wouldn't be the best idea. Not with the crown still latched onto you."

Sighing, Lily put her chin on his chest and looked up at him. "Do you think I'll ever be free of it?"

Roth leaned forward and kissed her forehead. "Knowing how strong you are, I have no doubt in my mind that you can do anything you set your mind to. Even breaking the hold of the Wicked Crown."

Lily hugged Roth tightly and sighed, sinking into his embrace once more. Of all the things that had happened to her over the course of the last few years, she had never expected to be trapped in Hell. Though, she supposed if anyone was going to be locked away somewhere, at least it was with her mate. She'd miss Earth though. She'd miss movies and going to the mall. Oh, and getting coffee on the way to class.

She let out a breath of dismay that had Roth peering down at her once more.

"What's wrong?"

Lily arched her brow and Roth clarified, "I mean besides the obvious."

"I was just thinking of all the things

I was going to miss about Earth. The biggest being coffee." Lily sat up and leaned her chin on her knee, letting the sheet pool around her waist.

Roth shifted to sit beside her, his lips pressing a kiss to her shoulder. "You know we have coffee here, right?"

Lily shook her head. "But it's not the same. Your coffee isn't even close to the deliciousness that they have perfected on Earth. Plus, there's movies and theaters and computers and oh, I could go on and on!" She hugged her knee tightly to her and tried to hold back the tears of frustration that threatened to fall. "I just don't know what to do. I know what I should do, but the thought of it makes me want to vomit."

Brushing her hair away from her neck, Roth wrapped his arms around her and placed his face near hers. "Sacrifice wouldn't be called a sacrifice if it was easy."

"Easy for you to say," Lily bumped back into him. "You can come and go as you please. While I'll be stuck here...forever."

"Not exactly," Roth drew out. "The only way to make it so that you cannot take off and try to conquer other worlds again is to lock the Underworld down. As in, make it so that no one, not even you, can get out or in."

Lily drew up sharply and turned to him. "That means whoever is on Earth won't be able to come back here and anyone here won't be able to get back to Earth...or Heaven." Lily chewed on her lower lip as she realized the sacrifice, she was going to make wasn't just for her but for everyone. "Can I really do that to them?"

Roth leaned back on his arms. "It's for the good of everyone. We will send out a proclamation stating what we plan to do and give them a set amount of time to decide if they want to live here or on Earth. Then when that time is up, we put the barrier up. There will be no portals, no way in or out. Ever."

"What if someone breaks it?" Lily inquired, trying to think of all the possibilities. "What if someone is strong enough to break the barrier and I'm unleashed upon the worlds again?"

Roth pushed up and pinched her chin between his fingers, drawing her face toward him. "Then I will do my best to distract you with all the new ways I can make you squeal." He kissed her then, so thoroughly that Lily almost completely forgot about what was to come.

"Oh my god, I'm going to miss you," Raven cried, hugging Lily so tightly that she feared she might not breathe again. "Are you sure you have to do this?"

Lily pulled away from Raven and smiled sadly. "Yeah, we think it's for the best. But hey, who knows, maybe someday I can figure out how to destroy that wretched crown and we'll see each other again!"

Raven gripped her hands tightly. "If anyone can, it's you! I'll be rooting for you."

"What about you?" Lily asked, turning the conversation back to Raven. "Are you sure you want to live on Earth...with him?" She jerked her nose toward where Ash was talking to Roth.

Raven smiled, the love clear in her face. "You know, he's not so bad, once you get to know him. I might even make an honest hellhound out of him some day."

Lily laughed and bumped her shoulder against Raven's. "Wouldn't that be a sight to see? Ash getting married! You'll have to send me an invi..." Lily trailed off and Raven frowned at her. "I'll be fine, I promise. Just take good care of yourself, okay?"

Nodding, Raven hugged Lily once

more before releasing her and going over to Roth and Ash.

Once Raven was gone, Lily turned and found herself facing her parents. Lilith and Lucifer. The two people in the world she wanted more than anything to be with and now that wasn't even going to be possible.

"Hey, baby girl." Lilith came up to her, her eyes brimming with tears. "Don't look at us that way. Everything will be alright. You'll see."

"But I just got you back and now I'm going to lose you all over again," Lily sniffed, trying to hold back the tears.

Lucifer brushed her hair behind her ear. "You'll never lose us. We're immortal. So even if it takes you a thousand years to break the hold of the Wicked Crown, just as it took me, then we will still be here...waiting for you."

Lily held her father's hand against her face for a moment longer before releasing it. "Where will you go?"

The two of them exchanged a look that held so much love in it that it made Lily's heart ache. Lucifer leaned his forehead against Lilith's and said, "I spent far too long away from your mother, I don't care where we go as long as we are together."

Lilith kissed him and smiled. To

Lily she said, "I've been around Earth a while and have found a few places I think your father will enjoy. So we'll travel around for a bit. Maybe we'll settle down somewhere by the ocean."

Lily giggled at the light that lit in Lucifer's eyes. "The ocean? I haven't seen an ocean in.... geez how many years has it been? Like a thousand years? Do they still have those big, huge fish that eat people?"

"You mean sharks?" Lily asked.

"No, no, ummm...." Lucifer stroked his chin as he thought. "One of them ate someone once in a story and you know of course God saved him and the fish spit him out."

Lily cocked her head to the side. "You mean, Jonah and the whale?"

"Yes," Lucifer snapped his fingers and pointed. "That one. A whale. Do they still have those?"

"Uhhh...yeah? They are kind of hard to miss." Lily laughed at the eagerness in her father's face. "However, I wouldn't go trying to get inside of one. They aren't like in the stories. They'll eat you, for real, and I need you guys safe for when I finally get out."

All of sudden the sadness poured back into her. She wasn't only losing her best friends but her parents too. Fuck. This was the hardest thing she has ever had to do. She didn't like it. Not at all.

"It'll be alright, love." Lilith cupped her face with her hands. "We won't be far and time will fly like that. Soon you'll have little ones of your own and you'll be too busy to miss us."

Lily leaned into her touch. "I doubt it. I haven't planned on kids for a long while."

Lucifer and Lilith laughed at her as if sharing some great joke before they shifted away so that Ash could come up to her.

"Hey, you," Ash fist bumped her shoulder. "How are you holding up?"

Lily gave him a weak smile. "Oh, you know, wishing I was back in English Literature right now."

Ash snorted. "That class was such a bore. Real life is so much more fun. Don't you think so?" He offered her one of his boyish grins.

"Could you imagine what Nathalie and the others would think if they knew what we were doing right now? That the freak girl was the Queen of Hell and you're marrying an angel?"

"Hey," Ash cried out, pretending to be offended. "I'll have you know, Raven is a Nephilim not an angel. Not fully anyway. She's part human."

"What's that mean in the long run?" Lily inquired with a smile.

Ash smirked. "That she's less prudish than her counterparts and far less self-righteous. Oh, the things I could tell you that we've done."

Lily held her hand up. "Please don't. I don't need any fresh nightmares. I have enough of those already."

Ash's expression softened and he wrapped his arms around her, giving her a tight squeeze. "It'll get better. Not any time soon but it will. One day you'll wake up and realize that the horrors that haunt you aren't quite so scary anymore."

Lily held him close and muttered into his chest. "I hope so."

"If not," Ash continued, withdrawing from her. "You can always use Roth to take your mind off of things. I'm sure he'd be more than happy to scramble that brain of yours."

"Hey!" Lily shoved him with a laugh as Roth came up beside her.

"Do I need to put you in your place before you leave, Blackwell?" Roth arched a brow at Ash.

"Nope, I'm good." Ash held his hands up in defense and slowly backed away. "I leave her in your capable hands. Be good to each other."

"We will be." Roth announced before turning to Lily. "Ready?"

"If I say no, can we not do it?" Lily asked, her voice cracking slightly.

"If that's what you want."

Lily stared up at him. "Really? You would stop this all if I wanted to? You'd spend every waking moment fighting to keep me here and away from other worlds?"

Roth brushed a tear that had streaked down her cheek. "If that is what would make you happy, then yes, I would more than readily do it for you."

Lily scowled. "Well, now of course I have to do it now. I can't let you be the more heroic of the two of us." Roth's lips ticked up slightly, a twinkle in his eye. "Stop looking at me like that, you're killing my concentration."

"Of course, my apologies."

Hands up, Lily tried to focus on making a ward just as Roth showed her and not on the faces of her friends and family as they disappeared into the nearby portal. This would be the final time she would draw on the power of the Wicked Crown. The final time she saw her friends and family before she locked her and the rest of the Under-world off from the whole of the universe.

As the power poured out of her, Lily concentrated on the good things to come. The flying lessons she was going to start with Roth soon. The new work that came with being queen. It was going to be a lot to get used to and perhaps some days she wouldn't even think of all she was giving up just as her mother said. Someday, someday everything will be normal. Or as normal as they could be for the Queen of Hell.

Raven

The dishes clinked in the sink as Raven finished up the wash from lunch. It was hard to believe it had been ten years since everything went down in Utopia. She never thought she would want the quiet life of a human. Neither she nor her mate were anywhere close to being normal.

Raven glanced out the kitchen window and smiled at the grown man playing tag with their two children.

Ash had taken to their human life far better than Raven had. He'd been more than delighted to find a normal boring job as an advertising executive. Going to work in the morning and coming home late in the afternoon to his family seemed to be everything he ever wanted in life. Of course, his coworkers didn't know what Raven knew.

While Ash may wear a suit and seem to be an average Joe, on late nights when they were feeling particularly cooped up in their new life, he and Raven would throw away their human personas and take to the woods and sky. Ash would run through the trees while Raven watched him from high above keeping an eye out for any hunters or onlookers.

Though, it was easier to hide what they were living just outside the city. Raven couldn't imagine trying to stay in the city where the buildings were so tightly pressed together that she had to go so high as an airplane could see her just to get any airtime.

There was a piercing squeal and their daughter, Michaele, took to the sky, her wings beating rapidly to hold up her little frame.

Raven sighed and wiped her hands on a nearby cloth towel. Still, while the neighborhood they lived in provided the much-needed freedom they needed, it wasn't Utopia. Or Underworld for that matter.

Opening the backdrop, Raven called out, "Michaele." The aforementioned froze in the air, startled. "You know you're not supposed to fly where the neighbors can see."

Shoulders dropping, Michaele slowly came back down to the ground, her hand holding onto the opposite elbow. "Sorry mom."

"Oh, come on, Raven," Ash grabbed a hold of their youngest, Wayne, holding onto the squirming child as he giggled. "No one is around. I checked."

Hands on her hips, Raven shook her head. "Still, you must be more careful. Humans are easily fooled into thinking we are good at dressing up but it would be hard to explain a seven-year-old flying ten feet off the ground."

Ash blew out a sigh and released their son, clicking his fingers in the air. "Your mom is right Michaele, better get those feet on the ground."

"Flying is cheating anyway!" Wayne stated with a growl.

"You are quite right, little man," Ash grinned and tousled Wayne's hair.

Michaele huffed and landed, tucking her wings away. "It's not my fault Wayne got the shit end of the stick."

"Language!" Raven reminded her and then to Wayne. "And your brother did not get the shit end of the stick. He's just as special as you."

"Language, mom," Ash teased,

earning a scowl from her. "And she's right. Wayne got my side of the family. Which is just as cool. If not cooler."

Michaele sniffed and put her hands on her hips and her nose in the air. "I don't see how changing into a dog is better. I don't want to get fleas."

"I don't have fleas!" Wayne shouted, stomping his foot at his sister. "Why would I want to have wings like a stupid bird? At least, I can run fast."

"So can I!"

"Nuh uh!"

"Yes, huh!"

Ash walked over to Raven and wrapped his arms around her waist, kissing her gently. "How's my beautiful mate today?"

Raven smiled. "Oh, you know. Living the dream."

Ash must have seen something in her expression because he cupped her cheeks and leaned his forehead against hers. "I know, baby. I miss them too."

"It's disturbing how well you know me." Raven pouted, leaning into his embrace.

"I'd be a bad mate if I didn't know you so well." Ash pulled back, brushing her hair behind an ear. "And I know you miss them because I miss them too. Every damn day."

"Oooo, language Daddy!" Wayne

called dramatically from two feet away making them jump.

"Holy hell, Wayne, wear a bell, would you?" Ash frowned down at the five-year-old boy. "And don't listen in on conversations or me and mom are gonna start kissing again."

"Ewww." Wayne made a face and pushed past them to go inside. "I'm hungry."

"You're always hungry," the little angel stated, chasing after him, not paying her parents any mind.

Raven rolled her eyes and exchanged a look with Ash. "Why don't you two go wash up for dinner?"

"Okay!"

The rush of little feet thudded down the hallway as Raven turned back to Ash. "Do you think they're okay?"

Ash rubbed his hands up and down her shoulders. "They're just kids. They'll grow out of it."

Raven pursed her lips. "Not them. Lily and Roth."

"Oh." Ash dropped his hands and stared off at nothing. "If I know Roth, he's got his hands full with keeping Lily in line. Besides they have a kingdom to lead. I'm sure they're too busy to get into too much trouble."

"I hope so." Raven sighed and

leaned her head against Ash's shoulder, breathing in his scent. "I'm just so worried about them. We haven't heard anything in ten years."

Ash wrapped his arms around her holding her tight. "Well, Lily did say forever. It's not like Hell has cell phones."

"They should," Raven grumbled into his shoulder. "Would make things easier."

"Yeah, but could you imagine the demons with cell phones? They'd break the screens with those big clumsy paws." Ash chucked, trying to break the tension.

Raven pushed away from him and smacked him on the shoulder. "Why did I marry such a weirdo?"

Ash beamed at her. "For my devilish good looks and massive cock, of course."

Raven snorted. "Oh yeah, sure, the biggest I've ever seen." She walked away with Ash following after her.

"What do you mean by that? Whose is bigger? Whose?"

Throwing her hands up in the air, Raven shook her head and lifted a prayer to whoever was listening. "Save me from the egos of men."

The waves crashed against the rocks off the shore of the little oceanfront house Lucifer stood in. The sun beamed down on him, happy to be able to shine so brightly.

It didn't know the one it shone down on was the former king of Hell. The sun shone for itself and did not care who saw it, only that it was the brightest star in the heavens.

Lucifer had once been that star. Not in the literal sense. His place in Utopia had been tenuous at the best of times but once upon a time he was the one everyone looked to for leadership and guidance. Now no one looked at him. Not even his own daughter.

"What are you doing over here sulking?" Lilith wrapped her arm around Lucifer's elbow. "We are literally in what the humans refer to as paradise and you have frown lines between your eyes. What worries you?"

Lucifer peered down at his wife, forcing a weak smile to his face as he patted her hand. "Just the usual. Nothing to bother you about."

Lilith lifted her head from his shoulder and pursed her lips. "She will be fine, Lucifer. Astaroth is there and he'll make sure that our baby girl is well taken care of."

"But that's our job," Lucifer

insisted, turning his gaze back out to the ocean. "We should be the ones taking care of her and we've already missed so much time."

Lilith let out a long sigh. "That's the hazards of being a celestial being, I'm afraid. We gave up time with our daughter to keep her safe. Now we have to trust that we did the right thing and let her live her life. Just as she would want us to do the same."

Lucifer squeezed her hand slightly. "But how can I be happy knowing she's out of our reach?"

"Well," Lilith huffed, pushing away from him to walk to the open doorway, her thin white dress floating around her as she walked. "I'd like to think I had something to do with it. Now instead of moping around, I'm going for a swim." She pulled the tie on her dress and it fell to the ground displaying the bare body of a goddess. Lucifer's groin tightened at the sight. Peering over her shoulder with a coy smile, Lilith purred, "Coming?"

With an eager heart and cock, Lucifer hastened to disrobe, chasing after his gorgeous wife. All thoughts of his daughter in Hell pushed to the side...for now.

Pain slashed through her back as she hit the wall of the training room. Her wings shoved her off it before bulleting toward the man before her.

"Is that all you've got?" Roth smirked at her, his bare chest gleaming with sweat. "Aren't you the great daughter of Lucifer? I'd have thought you had more to you than this."

Growling, Lily swung a fist out at Roth, barely missing by an inch. Roth however did not. He grabbed her wrist just as it passed and twisted them around until her front hit the mat, Roth's knee pressed firmly into her back. "I think...I win, again."

Lily huffed and let herself relax into the sticky mat floor. "Fuck me."

Roth chuckled and lifted off her. "Perhaps if you win, I'll indulge you."

Lily's eyes narrowed. "Indulge me huh?" Quicker than Roth could react, Lily shoved up off the ground, using her wing to knock the smirking male down to the mat, before promptly sitting herself upon him.

"Now why did it take that to get you to show your full strength?" Roth asked, placing his hands on her hips.

Lily rocked her hips against his, delighting in the hardness beneath her. "Maybe if you'd stop testing me and start fucking me, I'd be more motivated."

Roth grunted before stilling her movements with one hand, the other he placed on her lower stomach. "Forgive me if I'm a little overprotective. It has been a while since we've had to worry about you in a fragile state."

Lily arched her brow. "At what point during my last pregnancy was I fragile?"

The training room door opened just as Roth was about to answer.

"Ew. Gross. Can't you two be like normal parents and at least pretend you aren't banging all over the house," a male voice groaned from behind her.

"Grayson," Roth announced, his eyes never leaving Lily's, "take your sister and go practice your flying maneuvers. Don't think I don't know you've skipping lessons." He shifted his hold on Lily's hips pulling her tighter against his erection. "I need to teach your mother a lesson."

The sound of fake gagging made Lily grin. Then a quiet female voice asked, "Does that mean what I think it means?"

"Yes, they're gonna have weird ass adult sex. Now go before I lose my lunch."

When the twins were gone, Lily

threw her head back and laughed. "You really are too cruel to them. If anyone is teaching anyone a lesson, it's me teaching you." To prove her point, Lily used her magic to grab a hold of Roth's wrists and pinned them to the mat. With a salacious grin, Lily leaned down until her lips were millimeters from Roth's. "I win."

Roth murmured into their kiss. "That you do, my queen. That you do."

Erin Bedford is an otaku, recovering coffee addict, and Legend of Zelda fanatic. Her brain is so full of stories that need to be told that she must get them out or explode into a million screaming chibis. Obsessed with fairy tales and bad boys, she hasn't found a story she can't twist to match her deviant mind full of innuendos, snarky humor, and dream guys.

On the outside, she's a work from home mom and bookbinger. On the inside, she's a thirteen-year-old boy screaming to get out and tell you the pervy joke they found online. As an ex-computer programmer, she dreams of one day combining her love for writing and college credits to make the ulti-mate video game!

Until then, when she's not writing, Erin is devouring as many books as possible on her quest to have the biggest book gut of all time. She's written over thirty books, ranging from paranormal romance, urban fantasy, and even sci-fi romance.

Follow her on social media:
Website | Facebook | Twitter | Instagram | Newsletter | Facebook Group

May Sage is a geek, who much prefers getting lost in fictional world than dealing with reality. She's been writing since she was eight. As a little girl, everyone told her becoming an author was practically impossible, but she's a Capricorn, so she turned around and said "watch me."

She has various fur babies—a German Shepherd, two savannahs, and an adorable something-or-other with puppy dog eyes.

Her greatest aspiration is writing characters that make people want to throw their books at walls and wail in despair, or laugh hard enough to consider reading as an abs workout.

You can stalk her
at: Facebook | Instagram | Website | Newsletter | May Sage's Coven on Facebook for news, giveaways, and fun stuff <3